THE STORY COLLECTOR'S ALMANAC

NOTHING IN THE MIST

E.S. BARRISON

E.S. Barrison
www.esbarrison-author.com

Publisher's Note: This is a work of fiction. Names, characters, places, and incidents are a product of the author's imagination. Locales and public names are sometimes used for atmospheric purposes. Any resemblance to actual people, living or dead, or to businesses, companies, events, institutions, or locales is completely coincidental.

Content Warning: This book is rated 14+ due to violence, death, and alcohol use.

Book Layout © 2017 BookDesignTemplates.com

Nothing in the Mist/E.S. Barrison. -- 1st ed.
ISBN 979-8-9873602-5-5

To Kaina
Knoll
Hutch's Creek
Newbird Arm
To Heims Norte
The Capitol
Maedee's Outlook
Ab Aeterno
Grover's Marsh
Opal's Canyon
To Rosada
Stilette
To Volfium
To Heims Sur
To Proveniro
To Perennes
Janis

See a more detailed map in the back of the book.

The Council of Mist Keepers

NINGURSU
The God of Death

AELIA
The Healer

TOMAS
The Peacemaker

JULIETTA
The Painter

JIANG
Null

MALAIKA
The Cartographer

ALOJZY
The Architect

CAROLINE
The Illusionist

BRENT
The Story Collector

AL•MA•NAC

a publication containing astronomical or meteorological information, as future positions of celestial objects, star magnitudes, and culmination dates of constellations.

FOREWARD

People say that no story is unique.
Every story has been told.
None should be a surprise.
But I know differently.

Even after all these years, stories still surprise me. With every tale, every history, I am pulled in another direction, unraveling mysteries beyond my wildest dreams. Yet, no other story has amazed me like that of Jiang Mǐn.

Before I continue, I would like to note that for this narrative, I shall refer to him by his family name—the name he chose upon joining the Council of Mist Keepers.

Upon meeting Jiang, he belittled me with his first breath before returning to his drunken stupor about the Library. When he encountered those that I love, his anger sent them flying off balconies or collapsing into walls. There he stood, in the Council of Mist Keepers, as the loyal servant to that pernicious "God" of Death, Ningursu.

But behind his actions, I uncovered a story that tugged at my own heart. While his story does not absolve his behavior by any means, it helps to explain it. This is a story of a man who had found happiness, who found love, and who found purpose...only for a powerful evil to yank it from him.

All because he was in the wrong place at the wrong time.

The story sounds familiar in parts. I never thought I would see eye-to-eye with Jiang, but as his story enchanted me, I came to respect our similarities. We are both pawns in a game, manipulated by wrong choices, indecision, and powerful figures.

I can only hope that I can rewrite the tale for myself.

Because I must remember one thing.

I am the Story Collector.

And I will write my own ending.

-   Brenton Rob Harley
Ninth Member of the Council of Mist Keepers
The Story Collector

 ONE

Jiang Mǐn arrived in the City of Tencauri with nothing but his name. He wandered through the city streets, towering over the bustle of the city folk. They eyed him as he marched through the streets, with children whispering to their mothers and adolescent boys pointing in his direction.

Scowling, Jiang quipped at them, "What? You never seen a short giant before?"

At his remarks, the adolescents fled back into the alleys and corners. Alone, Jiang continued his walk, a stranger in a foreign city in a faraway land.

He'd traveled for weeks, leaving his home of Zhī Zhjùrén in Sīchóu Shíyóu after being denied service to the military. The youngest son of General Jiang Aiguo, everyone had expected him to follow in his father's and brothers' footsteps. Upon arriving for recruitment after the autumn equinox, the colonels laughed at his arrival.

"You? Join the military? Son, you would be squashed." One colonel had said to him, patting Jiang on the head with a chuckle.

"The military is for giants. Not you." Another colonel remarked.

Jiang begged for their acceptance, pleading to show off his strength and agility, but to no avail. He had spent years preparing, studying with tutors and teachers to make him wiser while working with his brothers to reach peak physical shape. It didn't matter. The Sīchóu Shíyóu military sent waves of fear from the eastern coast of Delilah and to the northern borders of Yilk. Armed with the strongest giants and the most cunning warriors, there was no place for Jiang—a giant hindered by his shorter stature.

Sure, as he arrived in Tencauri, he still towered over most patrons. But what was a 'short giant' in matters of war? What did it matter if he had wit and guile when the opposing Yilkan forces could crush him with a single step?

Shameful, guilt-ridden, and crushed, Jiang accepted the rejection and wandered with nothing more than his name.

He didn't return home.

He didn't face his father's disappointment.

Nor did he face his mother's tears.

Only once did he pause to say his final prayer at the altar of Xiao Gui—for good health to his family and long life to his brother, Li Jie. *Let them see glory before they meet you in their death. May you rescue their souls in their final sleep.*

With the prayer on his tongue, he left his home, left his country, and left his beliefs.

Only to arrive three weeks later with a caravan approaching Tencauri.

Now, with no destination in mind, he entered the city. A palace served as the pinnacle point of the city. It bore down from its hilltop on the streets below, with its fortifying donjon serving as a watchful eye, basking in the orange rays of sunset.

Jiang glowered at it. *You're not so impenetrable. Someday, we will come for you. Tèrén Zhī will belong to us again.*

Jiang carried with him the truth of Tencauri. His father's last stand before retirement took place within these walls. He had held the city for hours, wearing its old name like a flag, defending its ports and the people cowering in their houses. Yet even his army could not stop the flood of Yilkan soldiers marching forward, bearing the sun-shaped insignia on their chests. Sīchóu Shíyóu had giants, but Yilk's were taller.

And because of that, the city fell. But at its core, it would always belong to Sīchóu Shíyóu. It would always be Tèrén Zhī. Not Tencauri.

And never a product of Yilk.

Not that Jiang could do anything about it.

Here, he was nothing more than a commoner. A mere refugee brought by a nameless caravan with nameless people. He had but ten ingots in his pockets and a small sword at his hip.

With a huff, Jiang kept walking, his head down, not paying attention to where he walked. Only a thick whiff of tobacco pulled him from his reverie, directing his attention to a brightly painted building on the corner of the road. Patrons gathered out front, all dressed in brightly colored clothing. When they opened the door to the building, plumes of smoke exited, drifting around the feet of the patrons. They laughed at once, then entered the building.

Jiang approached as the door closed, eyeing the Yilkan text on the wall. He squinted as he read the words. "The Kursaal..." he licked his lips, trying to recall his studies. "A gambling house?"

He scanned the colorful building again. Back home, they outlawed gambling houses long before Jiang had been born.

But now...

He placed his hand on the doorknob. Guess it won't hurt to look.

With the turn of a knob, the smoke pulsed around him and lured him forward into temptation.

TWO

The Kursaal reeked of smoke and liquor. Jiang ducked into the entranceway, wrinkling his nose as he entered. Droves of individuals gathered around the tables, throwing hands of cards and rolls of odd-shaped dice across the surface. Jiang had no interest in such monotonous games and instead lurked over to the bar. The array of liquors reminded him of his father's cellar, where he and his brother, Li Jie, would sneak into at night, taking a taste of the liquid treasure.

An old barkeep glanced up as he approached, smiling with a mouth full of gold.

The barkeep spoke in Yilkan. Upon seeing Jiang's confusion, he switched first to Koa, then settled on Sī yǔ.

"Well, you're a face I haven't seen before," the bar-keep said in Jiang's native tongue.

"Not from around here," Jiang grumbled.

"Figured by your confusion. Here, let me get you a drink. My treat for the newcomer."

Jiang glanced around the Kursaal. Everyone held glasses of wine and mugs of beer in their hands, laughing and rejoicing. With their liquor came their vices; smoking, flirting, and touching.

"One drink, and then what? I become one of them?" Jiang glanced at the barkeep.

"I trust you are wiser than most of these drunkards," the barkeep continued smiling, "I'll get you my best cabernet. Give me a moment."

Jiang eyed the barkeep as he removed a bottle from the wall and popped open the cork. The barkeep poured it with silent ease, allowing the viscosity to settle and sit in the glass like a perfect sculpture. It swished along the glass as the barkeep placed it before Jiang.

"My very best, I promise. A cabernet from the Petla. The grapes only grow once every five years."

Jiang sniffed it once. The subtle, earthy tones did little to enchant him. He raised the liquid to the light. Despite its color, in the light, its consistency faded, allowing him to clearly see the candle flickering on the candelabra above him.

He brought it to his lips and let it slip over his tongue.

Then scowled.

"This might be a cabernet, but it's not from Petla. This watered-down Spinozan cabernet might work on your drunkards, but not me." Jiang shoved the glass away. "If you think this will win my business, you need a new strategy."

The barkeep smirked and removed the glass. "I think you're the first person since I bought the Kursaal to notice. You must have a good tongue there."

"I know good wine."

"Hm, very well. Here." The barkeep removed another bottle and filled a glass. The earthy aromas breathed from the glass.

Jiang took a sip and relaxed into its embrace. "Better. Still not a Petla cabernet, but close enough."

"Where's it from then?"

Jiang tasted the wine again and frowned, "Khov."

"Impressive," the barkeep remarked.

"If you insist. It's not that complex a science."

"I always thought of wine as an art...or even a type of magic."

Jiang shook his head. "Art implies there is no correct answer. Science acts solely as a fact."

"And magic?"

"Magic? It makes a mockery of both."

"Sounds like you were raised as an intellectual." The barkeep continued to press, smirking.

"I attended school." Really, growing up, he couldn't roughhouse with the other children, so he indulged in his studies. Smaller than the rest, his studies provided him with options and a future.

But, as he grew, he still ended up following behind his father, all in the name of his legacy.

"So you use this so-called science to determine the properties of the wine?"

Jiang shrugged and sniffed the glass again. "The elements are there. It is just differentiating them."

"Fascinating," the old barkeep pulled out a fresh bottle of wine. "Here, have another glass, my friend. On me."

THREE

The barkeep gave Jiang a room for the night after another four glasses. As Jiang drank, he could feel his tongue slipping, the formalities dropping, and the truth spilling. In a drunken stupor, he unraveled to the barkeep about his father's extensive cellar of wines, his years of studying to join the army and his inevitable rejection. If he gave his name, he didn't remember, nor did he recall the barkeep's name.

He woke with his head pounding like a drum on a thin mattress in a musty room. Squinting, he pulled his hair away from his face to take note of his surroundings. The room lingered with smoke from the Kursaal while the blinding light of midday battered against the window.

He cursed under his breath and stumbled from the bed, following the doorway into a thin hallway. With one hand against the wall, he staggered towards the small kitchen.

A tall woman stood in the kitchen, back turned, her long black hair falling to her waist. She didn't turn at first, catering to a teapot on the wood-burning stove. Jiang cleared his throat, and the woman spun around to face him. Her deep blue eyes caught Jiang at once. They locked onto his face, and for a moment, every thought fled his mind. He could only describe this woman as stunning.

"So you're the stray that Father let stay here, hm?" she asked, placing her hands on her hips.

The spell broke, and Jiang responded, "Oh, so you're the barkeep's daughter?"

"Yes. I suppose you don't remember meeting last night."

"I remember none of it."

"You were quite a drunk."

"Well, I apologize for my behavior. I shall take my leave." Jiang turned.

"Wait! Father wanted to speak to you before you left."

Jiang scowled. Why should he trust this sleuthing barkeep?

The woman continued, "He found you fascinating last night. That's unusual for Father. He thinks most of his customers are delinquents looking for quick pleasure."

"How do you know I'm not a delinquent?"

"Father has a good sense of trust."

"Maybe you say that to all his patrons. A pretty face like you surely lures everyone into a trap like this, so you can steal or kill...or whatever it is you Yilkans do." Jiang grunted. There was no reason to trust this woman. She probably saw him, a lone member of the Sīchóu Shíyóu army; now, she trapped him in her home, and she could turn him over to their authorities.

Jokes on her. I know nothing.

"What? You think I am a siren?" The woman asked.

"A siren?"

"You have never heard of a siren?"

"Sounds like a made-up word, if you ask me."

"It's a legend. That's all. But I guess an *intellectual* like you has no time for stories," the woman scoffed. "Stay here. I'll retrieve my father. This is not a *trap*."

The woman marched back down the hallway, hitting her shoulder against Jiang as she disappeared.

He grunted and rubbed his arm, glowering after the young woman. As she walked, her hips swayed, her long black hair like a cape behind her. She was a tall woman, for someone not of giant blood at least, the top of her head nearly touching the door frame as she entered another room.

"A siren..." he muttered to himself. He wracked his brain but could not recall the word. When he was little, his mother used to tell him legends passed down from parents to children. But, as he grew, his interest disappeared from such ridiculous stories. Far more important things lingered in the world. Stories would never answer the burning questions. They were fun for children, but no one else.

Just like magic.

The barkeep had mentioned magic down in the Kursaal, hadn't he? Jiang couldn't quite remember. The mere idea of magic made him cringe. It defied everything in his studies; sure, he had seen pyromancers and metallurgists and enchanters take control of the elements. But how? It didn't make the slightest bit of sense.

His father used to rant about magic in the confines of the home. "It needs to be controlled. Our army can tend to it, I am sure," he would say over a glass of wine. The Sīchóu Shíyóu army did have its own battalion of magic users; if Jiang had magic, it would have guaranteed him a spot in the army.

But no.

He was a small giant with no magic.

And now he stood in some musty house above some disgusting Kursaal in an enemy city.

The whistling of a kettle over the wood-burning stove tore him from his reverie. As if on cue, the barkeep entered the room, a grin wide on his face.

In the daylight, Jiang noticed how frail the barkeep appeared. He bore confidence down in the Kursaal, hiding the lines of age and the graying hair of experience. But in the daylight, his age stained him, blending him into the shadows.

"I thought you would sleep the day away," the barkeep joked as he removed a pot of tea from the stove. "I imagine the trip from Zhī Zhjùrén was tiring, hm?"

Jiang didn't respond.

"Oh, come. You spilled your secrets last night. No need to get so stone-faced now."

"I was inebriated."

"Yes, but what is done is done. You told your tale. There are no secrets. Here," the barkeep placed a cup of tea in front of Jiang. "This will help."

"Why should I trust any of the drinks you made for me?"

"I didn't make this tea. Kikyo did."

"Kikyo?"

"My daughter."

"Oh. Right," Jiang scowled at the cup again. The siren.

"I trust you'll be able to taste if it is made wrong." The barkeep winked as he took a cup for himself.

"I don't have a taste for tea," Jiang pushed the cup away. "As much as I appreciate the hospitality, though, I must leave."

"And go where?"

"Somewhere."

"That is not a good answer."

"I'll find a way. It is what I must do."

"Well, I might have a solution for you. Please, stay for a moment. I have a proposition."

Jiang huffed. His headache forced him to oblige.

The old man continued, "I would like you to become my apprentice."

"What?"

"Become my apprentice vintner."

"A vintner?"

"A wine connoisseur and merchant, for lack of a better description. That is where I got my start before running the Kursaal."

Jiang raised his brow. He'd never heard of a vintner before, nor had he ever considered becoming a merchant of any sort.

"A man with a talent like yours shouldn't let it go to waste."

"Talent?"

"Your perfect taste for wine, of course."

Jiang chuckled. *Ridiculous.*

"I promise, if you succeed, you'll be a very rich man," the old barkeep leaned forward, "quite rich indeed."

"And why should I trust you? I do not even know your name."

The barkeep grinned. "We exchanged names last night. You're Jiang."

"And you are?"

"Me? I'm Botan Habiki." The barkeep kept grinning as he spoke. "So...will you accept my offer?"

FOUR

Master Botan welcomed Jiang as his new apprentice. Reluctant at first, Jiang tentatively accepted, interested in Master Botan's trade. He had left his home with no prospects, and now, just because he used to sneak into his father's cellar, fate gave him a second chance. His father, no doubt, would have judged such a new venture. But with so little left for him, what choice did he have? At least here, he had a chance to be something.

Even if it was to become a glorified barkeep.

Jiang still talked little with Master Botan. He followed the old man to the markets, where he engaged in trades with different importers on the riverbanks. There, Jiang helped him retrieve cases of wine, which they sampled back in the apartment above the Kursaal.

While they tasted each case, Master Botan quizzed Jiang on the different aromas, flavors, and viscosity. To take over the Kursaal, Master Botan explained, Jiang needed to pass a test in a year's time. Then, and only then, would Jiang be ready. So he constantly quizzed Jiang, and by the end of each night, it left Jiang's head spinning, and he slinked back to his room often without finishing his meals.

Despite Master Botan's hospitality, he kept his distance, particularly from Master Botan's daughter, Kikyo. The young woman left each day after brewing a cup of tea to run errands for her father. She would toss a glower in his direction, then disappear through the door, her long black hair like a cape behind her. She only ever spoke to her father in Koa. While Jiang knew some Koa, he could only ever understand pieces of what the father and daughter said; he assumed they had to be whispering of him.

Yet Master Botan showed no resentment to Jiang. He put Jiang to work with a proud grin. The old master taught Jiang not just about the wines and the trade but about Yilk—from culture to formalities and even the language. Jiang did not retain everything, but the language became his new tool for success. In the evenings, when Jiang worked the Kursaal, knowing Yilkan gave him more ways to grow. In the Kursaal, Jiang learned the different games of chance performed on each table. Master Botan had hired the best dealers in the city, each dressed in formal robes and mystical masks, to hide their identity.

Often, the house won.

That, Jiang soon learned, was the true financier of the Kursaal.

Gambling fascinated him on a different level; while there was no faith or magic behind it, there was science and mathematics. Jiang watched as each gambler whispered their prayers, taking note of the probability of each win. Those who succeeded hailed their gods. But Jiang knew that it all came down to mathematical probabilities.

If he was a gambling man, he might have played the game.

Instead, he kept to the liquors and wine. When uncorking each bottle, he sampled each one, mastering the different tastes within the collection.

Master Botan had a selection of watered-down varieties he used for those too inebriated to make wise choices. The fanciest of wines, Jiang discovered, went to those deemed worthy of such delicacies.

Only Master Botan decided who deserved that label, though.

When not training beneath Master Botan, Jiang ventured to the fields outside of the city to practice his combat with the trees. All those years of training still vibrated in his soul. Even if he was not an official warrior, he would carry his father's words, his brother's swords, and his mother's praise.

Fight.

Survive.

Win.

And now, he had a new battle: win Master Botan's prize.

Win the tavern.

Win the trade route.

And win success.

After a couple months of studying under Master Botan, the old man cornered Jiang in the small kitchen with a single piece of parchment. He handed it to Jiang. Yilkan text scrolled across the page.

"What's this?" Jiang asked.

"Read it."

Jiang squinted at the text, slowly translating each word to himself.

"A...trader is requesting your presence?"

"That's right."

"So?"

"So I want you to go meet him."

"What? Without you?"

"Think of it as your first test. Secure the trade."

"But if I lose it, then you'll lose the business."

Master Botan chuckled. "I trust you will do fine, Jiang. And even if you fail, this trader always comes crawling back. I've gotten him angry quite a few times myself."

Jiang scowled at the paper again.

"He hails from Leega. Short man who goes by the name Witbooi. He's fluent in Yilkan but prefers to be addressed in the Leegan formalities. Do you remember what that is?"

Jiang wracked his brain over his studies. "Meneer, yes?"

"That's right. Witbooi is often blunt and quick. Don't let him swindle you, understood?"

"Yes, Master Botan."

The old man smiled. "Very good. Meet Witbooi at Dock Seven. Don't give him any more than thirty knots for the lot. If he asks for more, no deal. We won't make a profit that way."

"Understood."

"Good."

Jiang took a bundle of golden knots from Master Botan, then, with his bottle opener on his belt, left the apartment.

The streets of Tencauri bustled in the summer air. Upon leaving, Jiang pulled his long hair back and rolled up his sleeves. He headed to the port without listening to the babble in the street. The river circumnavigated the city, where boats traveled from the north and south, delivering food and delicacies from the countries of Delilah, Spinoza, Leega, Berusia, and even Koai. Yet Yilk had placed a trade embargo on Sīchóu Shíyóu, and obtaining exports like blue-feathered duck meat and golden quail egg were rarities.

But Jiang didn't have time to think about his old favorite meals. Rather, he focused only on Dock Seven, where a small boat decorated with multicolored flowers waited. There, a stout man with a curly mustache waited, sitting on a case of wine.

"Hullo!" The man jumped as Jiang arrived. "Oh—you aren't Botan."

"Master Botan sent me in his stead," Jiang remarked.

"I see." The man toyed with his mustache as he examined Jiang.

"Are you Meneer Witbooi?" Jiang asked, taking care to pronounce his Yilkan with ease and use the Leegan formalities.

"That is me, yes. You are Botan's apprentice?"

"That's right."

"Well then, do I have a delicacy to share with you!" The man hopped from the crate and opened it. Inside, bottles of deep red wines greeted them. "These here come from Effluvia. You know about Effluvia?"

Jiang shook his head.

"They're far east of here, across the sea. Some call them the Smoke Lands."

"You mean Gonvernnes?" Jiang asked. Sīchóu Shíyóu had a trade route across the sea with the nation, acquiring a variety of herbs and flowers grown from their luscious gardens.

"No, no. They are north of Gonvernnes. Uninhabited land."

"It's clearly inhabited if they make wine."

"Well, yes, there are nomads, but no one lives there long term. The mist there is thick and deadly. This here wine, it comes from a grape that grows only in those smoke-riddled mountains." The trader continued to ramble, "It makes a fine wine. One that will surely make your patrons proud."

Jiang removed a bottle, holding the murky wine up to the sunlight. This doesn't look that special.

"I am asking for fifty knots for the lot."

Jiang chuckled, "Now, I don't think any wine is that special."

"I promise, it is."

Jiang continued to examine the pale purple liquid. Before the trader could stop him, he removed the bottle opener from his belt and popped the cork from the bottle. With a swift movement, he sniffed the liquor once.

Then scowled.

"What are you playing at, Meneer Witbooi?"

"I'm sorry?"

"The earthy aroma, the pale red color. This isn't anything special." Jiang brought the bottle to his lips and took a quick gulp. He scowled as the unctuous texture slithered down his throat. "This is a Spinozan pinot gris. Watered down with..." He smacked his lips. "Ale? Really, Meneer Witbooi?"

"Don't be ridiculous!" Meneer Witbooi squirmed as he rubbed his hands together. "This is a pinot noir from Effluvia, a delicacy that only the wealthy and royal ever taste—"

"This is a scam!" Jiang threw the bottle onto the dock. Glass exploded at his feet. He towered over the trader, his anger rising. "Do you take me for a fool, Meneer Witbooi?"

"No! Of course not!"

"Then do not try to sell me this lie."

"You don't understand! I did have Effluvia pinot. I really did! You see, I promised Botan I would bring it to him, and I never like to let a client down. But...but there was this man that ambushed me and forced me to hand it over. Don't know how he did it, but I couldn't say no to him. He wasn't even that intimidating! Here, I can describe him to you. He had a scar and—and—"

"Oh, don't give me your stories. You're wasting my time." Jiang stepped back from the trader, eyeing the crate again. "I'll still take this crate off your hands. I'm sure there's some drunkard who will drink this rot."

"Wait, really?"

"Yes. For ten knots."

"I won't get paid for that price!"

"I shouldn't be paying you at all. But Master Botan doesn't condone stealing."

The trader glanced around, then back up at Jiang. "What about twenty?"

"Not at all. Ten. Otherwise, you're dragging that crate elsewhere—and the next person who tastes that lie might not be so kind."

"What about for fifteen?"

"You aren't in a position to bargain, Meneer Witbooi. I highly suggest you accept my offer."

The trader stared up at Jiang, shrinking beneath his tall stature. For once, Jiang truly felt like a giant. *Good. Let this man crumble at my feet.*

With a huff, the trader finally agreed. Jiang dropped the gold knots onto the dock and hoisted the crate under his arm.

He had, no doubt, passed his first test.

FIVE

"Well, that was quite impressive," someone called as Jiang left the docks.

Jiang spun. A figure dressed in a painted wolf mask and a red cloak stepped out from behind the row house.

"Botan-san, what're you doing here?" Jiang snapped. He recognized the woman in an instant, her long hair still bellowing beneath her hood.

The figure removed the mask. Kikyo smirked up at Jiang, her blue eyes glistening against the sunset.

"Did your father send you to spy on me? Does he not trust my capabilities?"

"Oh no. He believed in you from the start. I am too nosy for my own good." Kikyo continued to smile as she spoke.

"Didn't anyone ever tell you to mind your own business?"

"My mother tried. It didn't really work." Kikyo crossed her arms. "You really put Meneer Witbooi in his place. He's a weasel, but Father does enjoy doing business with him. Usually, he pulls through—not sure if my father would have noticed his deception or not."

"Never trust your friends. They'll stab you at the first chance."

"And what about your enemies?" Kikyo asked.

"They'll at least be honest in their deception."

Kikyo shook her head, laughing.

Jiang groaned and shifted the crate beneath his arm. "Don't you have somewhere to be, Botan-san? Errands for your father, perhaps?"

"Oh, I am allowed to have fun every now and again."

"By spying on me?"

"By watching the world go by, listening to conversations—"

"So, by being nosy?"

"Hard not to be when you're me." Kikyo slipped her wolf mask back on her face and hopped a few steps forward in front of Jiang. She moved like a spider dancing on its web. Each footstep, each hop, it came with ease and confidence.

"What does that mean?" Jiang followed behind her, watching each of her movements.

"Oh, nothing. At least it doesn't mean anything to you."

"Humor me."

"You've already expressed your disinterest in magic. Why should I bother wasting my breath on it with you?"

*Magic...*Jiang watched as Kikyo jumped to another stone. "You don't have magic. You're toying with me."

"Oh, but I do." Kikyo turned to face him, removing the wolf mask once again so their eyes locked. Jiang's stomach churned as her gaze bore into him.

"No, you don't," Jiang whispered.

She laughed. "Think about it. How did I hear you talk to Meneer Witbooi when I was by the boathouse?"

"I assume I spoke loudly."

"Even then, you faced away from me, so your voice carried forward across the river...not backward. It's simple science."

"Then you were closer than you appeared."

"Or my hearing is not like a human's at all. Perhaps it has been enhanced by whatever magical forces exist in the air."

"Bull."

"Here, I'll prove it to you. I'll go over there, by that tree," Kikyo pointed to a tree far down the street. "Once

I'm there, whisper something. I am sure I'll say it back to you word-for-word."

"I'm not playing these games."

"It's not a game…it's an experiment! You like science, don't you?"

Jiang grumbled. "Fine. One experiment."

Kikyo kept grinning as she skipped to the tree, her long hair blowing behind her. Once she reached the tree, she waved her hands as if to say 'go.'

Jiang hissed, "Beautiful little annoyance…"

Kikyo flexed her fingers.

And that was all.

Nothing changed.

No magic sparks.

Nothing at all.

Then, she skipped back over to Jiang, talking at once, "Just because I'm shorter than you, it doesn't mean I'm little. You. Are. A. Giant."

"That—"

"And you're annoying, not me."

"Still—"

"But…" Her eyes met him, "Thank you for calling me *beautiful.*"

Jiang stepped back from her. "This proves nothing. Maybe I didn't speak quiet enough or—"

"Beautiful little annoyance. That's what you called me." She turned away from him. "I'll take it as a compliment."

"It's not."

"I think it is," she giggled, then pulled the wolf mask back over her face. "Come. Father will be excited to hear of your success."

Jiang groaned and repositioned the crate before following behind Kikyo as she skipped through the streets. The way she walked, it reminded him of a little girl...or an overenthusiastic dog. She would turn her attention to those walking by as if pulling on the strings of their conversation. *I guess the wolf mask suits her...however ridiculous.* Jiang kept a far enough distance so people did not think he was with her. If he was destined to be a well-regarded vintner, he could have them thinking he was involved with some childish woman.

While Jiang could have abandoned her and gone home on his own, the way she behaved was peculiar enough to keep him from leaving. For science, he decided to stay beside her. As Master Botan's daughter, she surely had secrets about the trade and the town.

So he followed Kikyo on the long path home, around the bends that circled the grandiose palace that once belonged to the rulers of Sīchóu Shíyóu. Now, with its golden statues, towering donjon, and red painted walls, and the sun-shaped insignia on its flags, no remnants of Tèrén Zhī remained.

Yet the history remained a constant whisper in the air.

The war between Sīchóu Shíyóu and Yilk had gone on for centuries. From what Jiang's father told him, it started when a wizard stole the children of the Nine Giant Dynasties. This wizard dragged these children into the heart of Yilk, to the City of Errat, and plunged the region into one-hundred years of darkness.

A war began.

Blood spilled across the continent.

But the children never returned home.

And the battle never ended.

For centuries, Tèrén Zhī withstood the Yilkan onslaught. It was beneath Jiang's father's leadership that the city held its final stand. But despite the general's efforts and the army's ongoing fight, Tèrén Zhī fell and became Tencauri.

Now, Jiang stood here before the conquered castle, with a forgotten story pulling him into its clutches. He shook his head at once. *We don't even know how much of that is true.*

Kikyo stopped beside him as well. She lowered her mask, eyeing the castle, her brow furrowing and her nose crinkling. Her fingers flexed for a second by her side.

"Interesting…" she murmured.

"What?"

"Shush. I'm listening."

"Where? In the castle?"

"If you be quiet, yes—but obviously, you don't care what they said."

"Try me."

She squinted at the castle.

"What, do you have magical sight now too?"

"No, just focusing. Shush…" She held up her finger. "Lord la Hale received a message from the king in Errat. They want him to turn ownership of this castle over to someone named… Othar. The lord isn't happy."

Jiang raised his brow, "Does that mean anything to us?"

"Not really. Lords change all the time…although Lord la Hale says that this Othar doesn't have the 'criteria' to be a lord, whatever that—oh!" Kikyo jumped from her spot. "Says he's some nobody who happens to have magic. But I'm guessing the king has his reasoning."

Jiang scoffed.

"What?"

"Does it matter?"

"No, but it's interesting, isn't it?"

"Perhaps...but that hearing of yours is gonna get you trouble one day," Jiang muttered.

"Well, it can be our secret...can't it?"

"You trust me with that?"

"I think I do," she smiled at him. She had this peculiar way with her eyes, of wringing him in with a single stare. It was calming, in a way, like she understood more about him than he ever dared to say.

But then she pulled back on that ridiculous mask and broke the spell.

SIX

With Jiang's first successful trade, Master Botan put even more responsibilities onto his shoulders. The next morning, Jiang found a pile of new books outside of his room. At breakfast, the old vintner told him to read those books thrice over until he could recall every type of wine and its flavors. With that mere order, Jiang took a plunge into the art of reading. During the day, he would follow Master Botan to complete trades at the dock, carrying a book in his pocket like some student at an academy. He would walk along the streets with his nose buried in the words, reciting them to himself.

At night, before the Kursaal opened, Jiang would sit at the bar, sampling the wines and identifying them solely on taste, color, or viscosity. At night, with sobriety fleeting, he would dream of the different flavors.

Only to start again the next day.

He could feel Kikyo watching his every movement. In the morning, as she prepared breakfast, she would flinch at each word he mumbled beneath his breath. With the texts only available in Yilkan and Koa, it took Jiang twice as long to understand. Not only did the books detail flavors, but the history of the trade route, stemming from Spinoza and down to Koai. Wine held value and, much to Jiang's disbelief, stories in its taste. At first, he noted the histories, but then one book provided whimsical tales of a woman who transformed into a bundle of grapes. All, without a doubt, works of fiction.

He cursed to himself as he struggled through the text one morning.

Kikyo glanced over from the pot of tea. "That's not a nice word."

"Mind your business."

"Do you need help?" She skipped to his side.

"No! I can read!" Jiang glowered at the page.

"You're still on page one."

"It's just a ridiculous story about how wine is the blood of...something. I don't know. It will not help me be a vintner."

Kikyo glanced over his shoulder. "Oh! The story of the slaughtered dryad! Yes! That's my favorite story. But..." She pointed at the first sentence. "This is in old Koa. If you weren't raised to speak it, I can see how it might be difficult to understand."

"Maybe I would understand it better if it wasn't so ridiculous!"

"Mǐn, it's okay if—"

"Do not call me Mǐn."

"I hate using family names, though. I know nothing about your family, so why shouldn't I call you by your given name?"

"My family name is everything. It is what we have always been and what we shall always be."

"Very well," Kikyo shook her head and returned to the text. "What I was trying to say, *Jiang*, is that it is okay if you are struggling with this text. Koa is my native tongue, and I struggle with this book. But I can help."

"I don't need your help," Jiang growled.

"Fine. Be like that." She returned to the teapot without that usual skip in her step.

Jiang huffed and returned to the book. He licked his bottom lip before mouthing the first line to himself. "She who was born by the...the..."

"The sap of a tree," Kikyo murmured.

Jiang glowered at her, but instead of saying a word, he resumed reading. "Wandered the grapevines of the…of the…"

"Paradise."

"She who was born by the sap of the tree wandered the grape vines of paradise." Jiang glanced again at Kikyo.

And she smiled.

With Kikyo's assistance, Jiang continued to pour over the books, allowing him to conduct trades and master the tastes during the day. In the morning and the late evening, he would read. At first, it started with Jiang reading out loud and Kikyo correcting him, whether or not he asked for help. In the kitchen, she would occupy herself with cleaning or sorting through her father's finances. She knew each story by heart, whispering them alongside Jiang.

Soon, Jiang found himself fumbling just to hear Kikyo's voice.

And slowly, outside of the books, they even began to talk. Kikyo told him how she had traveled with her father to Tencauri and how, growing up, she'd felt like an outcast. She had always been nosy, always been a little peculiar.

Just like a small giant in a land where height mattered.

And with that, Jiang slowly opened up to her about his life—training to be in the army, his abandonment of academic pursuits, and how he arrived in Tencauri himself. She listened with intent, and once he'd finished talking, she directed him to a story in the text.

"I don't understand why your father wants me to read these stories. They're not true." Jiang grunted one evening as they sat at the dining table.

"You'd be surprised what is true. I've heard many truths that sound imaginary." Kikyo flipped to the next page in the book. "But it might be valuable to learn these stories so you understand where the wine comes from. Think about it. If a Spinozan merchant came to you, unsure if he should sell you the fancy chardonnay, you could impress him with the story of the dragon riders of Graycott and their quest to find the golden grapes. Just imagine the shock they'd have, hearing that from you, some hulking figure with a dumb face."

"Dumb face?"

"Let's face it, you don't look like an intellectual."

"I find that quite rude, Botan-san."

"You called me a beautiful little annoyance." Her eyes twinkled.

"Because it is the truth."

Kikyo smirked, her cheeks turning a bright pink as she sat there beside Jiang. Her shoulder touched his arm. When did he allow her to get so close to him? The mere touch of her skin against his arm made his hair stand on its ends.

He reached for a cup of tea to distract him.

Kikyo redirected the conversation. "These stories, whether true or not, mean a lot to people. Understanding the stories means you'll understand your customers. Then, you can build a new dynasty."

Jiang scoffed, "And who will I build that dynasty with?"

"You'll be able to find a wife."

"As you said, I don't talk to anyone. How would I find myself a wife?" Jiang laughed.

"Women will flock to you once you're successful. Beautiful women! Annoying women! Amazing women!"

Jiang turned to her, observing her. "Sounds like you are describing yourself."

"I..." The pink in her cheeks deepened.

"You think I would want to marry someone like you?" Jiang asked.

Kikyo lurched from the table. "That's not important! I...I should go to bed!"

Before Jiang could stop her, Kikyo fled from the room, her long black hair billowing behind her into the darkness of the hallway.

SEVEN

Jiang couldn't sleep. He lay awake, tossing and turning, unable to focus. Weeks ago, the upcoming vintner test would have kept him awake. But now...now he kept seeing Kikyo, with her face red and abrupt departure. What had he said? He had asked a question! Nothing more! Why hadn't she said something like, "Well, no one else would want you"?

Why did she flee?

Kikyo had always been one for snarky remarks and playful flirtation. This time, it was different.

This time, it felt...real.

Does she actually have feelings for me? He rose from the bed and stared at his hands. Why did he care if she did or not? Then again, hadn't he spent time reviewing books that he didn't need to remember just to hear her voice?

Love. That was a pathetic idea. Back when he had plans to join the army, love was the last thing on his mind. He never flirted with the girls back home. Sure, he admired them from afar, but his focus had been on the army. Someday, he knew he would marry someone his father found suitable. But the idea of love? It never even occurred to him.

Until he recalled Kikyo's laugh.

And her bright-eyed smile.

He cursed under his breath.

What would Master Botan think? Would he accuse him of using Kikyo? Or would he welcome Jiang with a smile?

Either way, until Jiang quelled Kikyo's worries, he didn't have to worry about Master Botan's reaction.

He pulled on his robe and tiptoed from his bedroom. A dim light flickered from Kikyo's room.

This is just another test. I can do this.

Sweat gathered in his palms as he knocked on the door.

"Botan-san..." he called through the door.

No response.

"Botan—Kikyo. It's me," he licked his lips, "it's Mǐn."

The light flickered again beneath the doorway, followed by the creaking of the floor. After a beat, the door creaked open.

Kikyo stood in the doorway in a long, silken robe. She stared up at Jiang with bloodshot eyes. "I thought you said not to call you Mǐn."

"I changed my mind. *You* can call me Mǐn."

"Mǐn..." she whispered.

"Kikyo," Jiang replied.

He locked eyes with her. Neither of them moved. It was as if, with that single stare, all of Jiang's walls fell. Sure, she irked him...but there was something compelling about Botan Kikyo. She heard everything, listened to every word, and not only responded but took care with her insight. Her knowledge of wine and the world amazed Jiang. If she had wanted, Kikyo could have easily taken over her father's trade.

Kikyo's gaze fell to the floor. "I am sorry about earlier. I should have answered your question."

"Huh?"

"You asked why you would take a woman like me for a wife...and the answer is obvious."

"It...it is?"

She gulped, nodding as she said, "You wouldn't take someone like me...because you deserve someone better."

Jiang placed his finger under her chin and lifted her gaze to meet his eyes. Her pupils shook as he stared at her.

"You're right," Jiang muttered, "I wouldn't take someone like you."

She shrank.

But Jiang kept her from pulling away, "I wouldn't take someone *like you*...because I would only take *you*."

Her shoulders relaxed. When she opened her mouth, no words exited her lips.

Jiang placed a hand on her cheek. Her smooth skin, her wide blue eyes. They enchanted him as if a product of magic itself. Without a word, she leaned into him so Jiang could bring his lips to her mouth in a devouring kiss.

EIGHT

For the following weeks, Jiang and Kikyo kept their romantic plight a secret from Master Botan. During the day, they maintained their formal civility, leaving Jiang to pour over his studies without distraction. With Master Botan's test approaching, in the daylight, studying became a fixation.

But with the setting sun, his trance broke, and once Master Botan retired for the evening, he slipped into Kikyo's room. Despite sharing a bed for a passionate rendezvous, they never slept in the same room, leaving in the early morning so as to keepMaster Botan in the dark regarding their affair. In the privacy of their bedrooms, they whispered about their days before being derailed by passionate kisses and consequential touches. Jiang's obsession with wine fell to the back of his mind at those times, instead enamored solely with Kikyo.

"I heard that the wizard, Othar, arrived a few days ago with his daughters. The king's men had to drag Lord la Hale out, kicking and screaming. I could hear him from across town." Kikyo said a few nights before the vintner test, her head resting against Jiang's bare chest. "I'm curious to see what changes Othar will bring."

"He's probably supposed to hold off the Sīchóu Shíyóu army," Jiang muttered, running his hand through her hair while inhaling her peony-scented perfume.

"Not everything has to do with that silly war."

"Politics always has to do with war."

"I don't know. Lord la Hale said something about Othar bringing unworthy blood into the castle."

"Not that Lord la Hale is worthy either."

"Well, I'll keep listening for as long as I can," Kikyo said.

"Don't endanger yourself."

"I won't. I'm like a fox," she grinned at him.

"You wear a wolf mask."

"A wolf-like fox, then."

Jiang scoffed. *Silly girl.*

"I've been doing this since I was a little girl. Used to eavesdrop on my father's customer's downstairs. Once, I helped the authorities infiltrate a crime ring."

"Liar."

"No! I'm telling the truth!" She sat up in bed, her long hair hanging over her body like a cloak. Jiang wrapped his arms around her waist and pulled her close.

"And how will you prove it?" Jiang asked.

"You just need to believe me. Who knows...maybe my hearing will help stop that war you're obsessed with?"

"If you do that, then I'll start believing in all those silly stories you made me read." He recalled a story that he read about a Forest Queen who could move continents in Gonvernnes. Ridiculous as it may have seemed, that queen could stop a war with a single flick of her fingers.

"Now I have a motive," Kikyo laughed. "Too bad I won't be so foxlike much longer."

"What do you mean?"

The light in Kikyo's eyes wavered, and she climbed out of bed with a sigh. He took in every curve of her body. She was like a river, with perfect twists and turns, rippling with each breath. But as the silence hung, her current grew more powerful. Her face scrunched as she tried to find the right words.

"What is it, my beloved?" Jiang pressed.

She whispered as she pulled on her robe, staring at the closed window, "I missed my monthly. It should have come last week…but…it didn't. It has never been late."

Jiang took her hand. "So does that mean you are with child?"

"I will meet with the local midwife in two days. She will confirm the truth of it." Kikyo shrank as her confession continued to fill the room.

"You are with child…" Jiang approached her side. With a smile, he knelt before her, unable to contain a smile. He hadn't thought of a family ever in his life. But now, with Kikyo, he saw himself nowhere else.

"After the test, I shall ask your father for permission to marry you." Jiang squeezed her hands. "If you'll have me."

Kikyo's face illuminated. "I'll have you forever."

And in that moment, Jiang had everything.

NINE

While Jiang bubbled with the excitement of his unborn child, Master Botan's vintner test did not wait. Three days later, as the sun set in the sky, he kissed Kikyo once for good luck before venturing downstairs to the Kursaal. Master Botan waited for him at a small table. Around him, countless patrons gathered. Jiang eyed them as he approached Master Botan.

"What is the meaning of this?" he asked.

"You haven't noticed? You've been the talk of the Kursaal for weeks—they've all been placing bets on whether you'll pass my test."

"I am not some bull."

"But you are the first one to meet my standards. I have had others come, aware of my age and talents, to study beside me. You are the only one who remained committed and showed true skill. Now, you shall take my test...a test that not even my dear Kikyo can pass."

The mere mention of Kikyo's name made Jiang's stomach flip. He had to pass this test for her.

"Very well. I hope they placed their bets on me." Jiang glanced over the crowd one last time as he took his seat. He resisted the urge to smile upon seeing a figure in a wolf mask towards the back of the room.

He took a seat at the table. Before him sat three glasses of wine, shimmering in the dim light of the Kursaal.

"The test is simple," Master Botan said. "These three wines are pinot noirs. Your test is simply to identify where they originate from. Simple, yes?"

Jiang stared at the three glasses. Each bore the same deep red color, dark and murky as if filled with blood. With Master Botan's nod to begin, Jiang lifted the first glass, holding it to the light to watch as the liquid clung to the sides. The scent of oak and earthy minerals weaseled its way into his nostrils.

Then he brought the liquid to his lips. Earthy. Mineral ridden. A sharp twinge.

"An aged noir from São Caméliosa in Gonvernnes..." Jiang muttered.

"Correct," Master Botan said with a smile.

Jiang moved to the next one. This one had a taste of brimstone, with a certain bitterness lending itself to fire. After swishing it in his mouth, Jiang placed the glass back on the table. "A young noir from Graycott in Spinoza. I thought you would try to stump me more, Master Botan."

The old vintner continued to grin. "Well, I had to throw an easy one in there. But this last one, well, if you identify it, then I'll happily turn my Kursaal over to you."

"And after that...what will become of you?"

"I think my dear Kikyo and I will return to Koai. It has been far too long."

"Koai..." Jiang froze, raising his gaze to find Kikyo in the back of the crowd. Even behind her wolf mask, he could feel her eyes on him. *It's now or not at all.*

"Well, are you ready?" Master Botan asked.

Jiang returned to his test, staring at the final glass. If he guessed wrong, Kikyo would stay here.
But he had worked too hard for this.

Kikyo would know he lied.

He had to ask before it was too late.

"Yes...but..." Jiang stammered, "I do have one question."

"Of course."

Jiang squirmed. He had not wanted to ask such an important question amid a crowd. But it was now or never…

All for his beloved Kikyo.

"Master Botan, your daughter and I have grown close over the past year," Jiang said.

"Ah, yes. She helps you study."

"Yes, but…" Jiang took a deep breath. "We're close. Quite close. And…I was wondering…" He glanced again towards Kikyo. "I was wondering if I were to pass this test, if she could stay here with me. As my wife."

A beat passed.

Then, Master Botan's smile grew. "You wish to marry my Kikyo?"

"Yes, I do."

"You do not have to pass this test to marry her."

"But I need to be able to provide for her." *And for my unborn child.*

"Well, no matter the outcome, as much as it pains me to leave her, your wish is granted. You may marry if that is what you both want."

"Thank you, Master Botan. It is." Jiang kept his gaze on Kikyo. Beneath the mask, she could not contain her grin. She hopped on the soles of her feet, bouncing like a child.

Jiang resisted the temptation to run to her, lift her up, and kiss her in excitement. No matter what, he still had his everything.

If he passed the test now, it would be all the better.

He returned to the final glass, heart racing, giddiness filling his chest and throat. Without a doubt, it was another noir. As he lifted it from the table, the liquid swirled as if composed by the wind. A whiff of smoke and berries filled his nostrils.

And with a taste, it was like he was soaring through the clouds.

He smacked his lips together.

"I never thought you would find one of these, Master Botan." Jiang returned the glass. "This noir is quite old, right? And from far away?"

"Yes, but from where?" Master Botan pried.

"I can only assume it's from Effluvia. I'd say the grapes are from the smoke-riddled mountains, perhaps where the birds fly to in the summer." Jiang licked his lip. "Yes, without a doubt, this is a smoky noir."

Master Botan nodded once but did not speak. Jiang's stomach tightened. Did he get it wrong? Did he disappoint the old master? Would he take back his blessing due to Jiang's mischaracterization?

The old vintner turned to the crowd, watching intently from every corner of the Kursaal. "Well, if you placed your bets on my apprentice, it seems like you're going to leave today quite wealthy. He has passed my test."

TEN

Three days after the vintner test, Jiang Mĭn and Botan Kikyo married on the docks by the river in a private ceremony with only Master Botan and an officiant. Kikyo stood before Jiang, dressed in a silver-laced shiromuku with long lacy sleeves. Her long black hair sat on her head like a crown. Compared to her, in his old military uniform and torn leather, Jiang felt unworthy. But it did not deter his happiness, as he and Kikyo pledged themselves to each beneath the watchful eyes of Xiao Gui.

As the ceremony ended, he lowered his lips to Kikyo's forehead. "And I promise...to death and beyond."

"Until death and beyond," Kikyo whispered back as Jiang removed his lips.

With a mere promise, their marriage was sealed with a final prayer from the officiant.

"I wish you all the luck and health," the officiant remarked.

"Thank you," Kikyo replied.

The officiant took his leave with a bow, leaving Jiang and Kikyo with Master Botan. The old vintner's eyes sparkled with tears while a smile etched across his face. He placed his hand on Kikyo's shoulder.

"As much as I will miss you, my Kikyo, I am so glad that you found someone worthy of your love," Master Botan sniffled. "I wish you many years of love and prosper."

Kikyo took her father's hands. "Stay with us, Father. There is more than enough room in the Kursaal. Please."

"I already booked a boat to leave today—in anticipation of Mĭn's success. There is no place for me now that I've lost the Kursaal."

"Master Botan, I still have much to learn. You have not lost the Kursaal. It will always be yours." Jiang approached the old vintner.

"No, it is yours now."

"But—"

"My son, you will be fine. Kikyo has access to all my records, and you have been handling most of my trades over the last few months. I have no doubt that the Kursaal will thrive under you." Master Botan placed a hand on Jiang's shoulder. "I expect both of you to write to me."

"Of course, Father," Kikyo cried. Jiang reached over to wipe one of her cosmetic-stained tears from her cheeks.

Master Botan smiled at both Kikyo and Jiang, then glanced down the river. A curved wooden boat with a wide sail bobbed against the quiet water. Two sailors paddled at the front of the boat, directing it to the dock.

Master Botan picked his bag off the ground. "I believe that is my ride. It is time for me to return home."

Jiang stepped back, allowing Kikyo to embrace her father. She showed no remorse for her decision. After all, wasn't this how it had always been? Find a spouse, move away from home, and never return. Jiang's mother had undergone the same ordeal—her parents only visited from the south every couple of years; Jiang couldn't even remember their faces.

Master Botan kissed Kikyo on the head and stepped back, taking a gander at both Jiang and Kikyo. "Be proud and strong, my children. With that strength, you shall be everything."

Jiang held Kikyo close as Master Botan left on the boat, disappearing as a speck down the river. As time passed, new boats pulled into the dock, decorated with gold and scarlet. Soldiers gathered at their helm, casting scowls in the direction of any civilians loitering on the docks. The arrival signified a time to leave, and with hands interlocked, Jiang and Kikyo headed back to the Kursaal.

As they walked, Kikyo gripped Jiang's arm, wiping her nose with the back of her sleeve. She tilted her head slightly as they moved further away from the water. Jiang recognized this movement, like that of a dog listening to a distant storm.

"What do you hear, my love?" he asked.

She held up her hand, brow furrowed and nose wrinkled.

Jiang waited, letting her sit with her magic. He still admitted openly to her that magic still defied all his logic, but he appreciated its capabilities, especially now that Kikyo had showed him its power.

Finally, Kikyo snapped back into the present, "You saw those boats on the dock, right? The gold and red ones?"

"I do indeed have eyes," Jiang chided.

Kikyo scoffed. "Well, I wasn't sure if your mind was elsewhere."

"Oh? Like where?"

"You know exactly where." Her fingers fell on his back, tracing up his spine.

He shivered at her touch.

"But we can focus on that later," Kikyo pulled her hand away, "let's talk about the boat."

"Right, that boat." Jiang always found Kikyo's insistence amusing. She could bounce between topics without being prompted, pulling his attention in five directions during a conversation. "What'd you hear?"

"Just something peculiar, I suppose. It might mean nothing at all."

"Humor me."

"Well...remember when we discovered some sorcerer named Othar was replacing Lord la Hale?"

"Mhm."

"Well, from what I overheard, his lady friend...some woman named Solana, well, she arrived a few days ago."

"So?"

"Don't you find it interesting, Mĭn? I think more people are discussing her than Othar!" Kikyo skipped ahead a few paces. "I've heard some say that she is a powerful alchemist or sorcerer. People say she was born far away from here...in the Merton region, they say."

"So?"

"Well, it's not like we get many people from Merton. They're a different type of people there. In fact, that boat is delivering her water from the hot springs in the Mertoni territory. That's what the sailors were grumbling about, at least."

Jiang raised his brow. "Why would they bring spring water here? We've got plenty of fresh water."

"That's what the sailors were wondering! Seemed like a waste of their time, but it's what Solana wanted—and now that Othar has so much power, they have to listen."

"All because the king said he has power..." Jiang grumbled.

Kikyo spun around and poked Jiang in the chest. "Just a part of that war you're obsessed with."

"I'm not obsessed over it anymore. I have other things to care about," he grumbled.

"Oh? Like what?" She stopped at the edge of the path, mere steps from the castle gates.

He pulled her close. "I think you already know."

With Kikyo, the war didn't matter. The life of a soldier belonged to a past life.

It meant nothing to him.

Nothing at all.

Eleven

With Master Botan gone, Jiang resumed his duties in the Kursaal. For the first couple months, all ran as he expected; patrons would enamor themselves with the temptations of the Kursaal, purchasing their wine and liquor without a flinch. Kikyo helped him manage the finances, and each day he greeted traders on the docks, obtaining shipments from abroad. He knew the traders by name as well as the taste of their wine in his heart.

About three months into his tenure, Kikyo entered the kitchen as she did each morning, carrying her book of invoices and letters. Jiang smiled as she entered, the glow of pregnancy following her steps.

"Good morning, my love," he said as she sat at the table.

"Now that I can sleep, it certainly is a good morning," she said as she opened the book.

Jiang poured her a cup of tea and sat beside her, looking over her notations on the page.

"Profits are up?" Jiang asked.

"Yes—you're working magic with the traders...and I've overheard that patrons think the quality of alcohol has gone up."

"Which means they bet more?"

"And lose more." Kikyo flipped through the pages until reaching a small stack of letters. "We received some complaints, but I'll handle them. Nothing a free drink can't fix."

"If it's in our budget."

"I don't think we'll have to worry about our budget much longer." Kikyo pulled a letter from the back of the pile. Even with the envelope opened, Jiang recognized the broken seal of the sorcerer Othar. Sealed with the image of two triangles, reminiscent of an hourglass, it was hard to forget the sorcerer's brand.

Jiang took the letter from Kikyo. He skimmed over the page, taking care to read the Yilkan text.

To the reputable, respectable, and honorable Botan Habiki—

Word of your delightful wines echoes through our city. It did not take long for me to hear of your skill for acquisition upon my arrival.

As you know, I am betrothed to the lovely Solana Ali, and we intend to host a fantastic marriage ceremony in the coming months. No celebration is complete without a taste of wine.

That is why I am summoning you now to my court. I would like to sample your finest wines so that our patrons are smiling with utmost glee upon leaving.

Please deliver them presently. I shall be waiting.

Odo Othar

Jiang blinked as he read through the letter. The note had been for Master Botan, but that meant nothing. He owned the Kursaal—and thus, he was now Master Botan.

"Don't you see, Mǐn!? This will secure the Kursaal for years to come!" Kikyo exclaimed. "If we become the sorcerer's personal vintner, imagine—our children will never go hungry!"

"And we could create a new legacy…" Jiang murmured, then returned his gaze to Kikyo. He could give her a beautiful home; she'd never have to work again. They'd be able to hire others to work at the Kursaal, so they could sleep at night without a fret.

He never wanted to help the *enemy* of his home country.

But Jiang had made a vow: forever and beyond—he wore Kikyo's name as his banner.

TWELVE

Jiang spent all day sorting through a vast array of wines with Kikyo. They narrowed the selection down to four bottles: a bitter, ashen red from Spinoza, a sweet white from Merton, an apple wine from Delilah, and a smoky noir from Effluvia.

After loading the selection into a crate, Jiang kissed Kikyo on the cheek the next morning and ventured to the palace.

"I'll be listening, my love," Kikyo said, placing a hand on her stomach as she stepped away. "Go make us rich."

Her kiss still lingered as Jiang carried the crate up the hill towards the palace. Over the past year, the blatant stares no longer bothered him; some marveled at the fact he was a giant, while others mocked his height.

How could a giant be so short? It didn't matter to Jiang any longer.

Now, he would have the ear of the sorcerer.

Upon arriving at the gate to the palace, he presented the letter to the guard. With a single nod, the guard permitted him entrance and led Jiang up the stairs towards the entry hall.

Jiang expected to find himself surrounded by magic upon entering. Yet, with its drab red floors and golden walls, the palace was nothing but ordinary. Statues of previous rulers lined the walls, and paintings of war scenes and battles echoed from the paintings. Jiang kept his eyes moving, eyes forward, lips sealed. He only stopped once by a painting depicting a figure that reminded him of his father, kneeling over the bodies of fallen soldiers.

"Beautiful, isn't it?" A stern, feminine voice caught Jiang off guard.

Standing at the end of the hallway stood a woman draped in a golden dress. Thin, with a stern face and dark eyes, she eyed Jiang with a peculiar focus. There was something about her that made the hair on his arms quiver. Sure, she was beautiful, with her deep brown hair woven together like a lattice on her head. But, if magic had a sensation, then it must have felt like her gaze.

The woman continued, her accent resonating with a smooth hint of Mertoni, "A dear friend of mine painted all of these. If you look long enough, they appear to move."

Jiang turned back to the painting. "I don't see anything moving."

"Ah, not the imaginative type then," the woman joined his side, "this one is called *The General's Final Bow*. Have you heard that story...about how Yilk reclaimed Tencauri after a bitter battle?"

Jiang nodded.

"It's quite the tale, I must say. I am so happy that my dear Odo gets to lead this beautiful city now. He will provide a nice wall against...those giants."

The insult felt directed, but Jiang kept his lips pursed. A woman like this, with the Mertoni accent and determined stride, had to be a woman of power.

"I assume you are the sorcerer's betrothed, then?" He asked the woman, redirecting the subject.

"Yes, that is correct. Solana." She held out her hand.

Jiang stared at it.

After a momentary pause, Solana pulled her hand away. "So you must be the barkeep he contacted?"

"I prefer the term 'vintner.'"

"I see. Very well, then come. He is waiting." Solana motioned Jiang to follow her down the entry hall.

Jiang shifted the crate of wine in his arms and followed behind Solana. She moved like a regal queen, her steps careful and weightless. In a certain glimmer of light, it was as if smoke followed at her heels. But with it, there was no personality, no joy; perhaps before Jiang met Kikyo, he would have sought a woman like her.

But now...he needed his ray of light.

Solana opened the grand doors where the hallway ended. A bout of yellow smoke pummeled from the room, forming distant shapes against the walls. Jiang squinted once, and in that moment, the yellow gasp of smoke subsided.

In its place, a marble courtroom greeted him. The seats blended seamlessly in with the floor and wall. Other than the fading yellow smoke, the only color staining the room came from the individuals at the far end of the hall.

Jiang's footsteps echoed as he approached.

The man at the head of the room rose. Scrawny, with peppered hair and a misshapen beard, this was the last man that Jiang expected to be a powerful sorcerer.

"Ya must be Botan Habiki, aren't ya?" the man said.

"Uh, no," Jiang straightened his back as he spoke. "I apologize. Master Botan left a couple months ago and asked me to run his Kursaal in his stead. I promise the quality of our wine has not suffered."

"I imagine he trusted ya with a reason then, isn't that right?" The sorcerer leaned forward, his silver eyes glimmering on his narrow face.

"I believe so."

The sorcerer smiled. "Very well. What is ya name, then?"

"Jiang Mǐn, sir."

"Mǐn! Nice to meet ya, Mǐn-boy!" The sorcerer jumped down from the platform and approached him. The two other figures—teenage girls, from what Jiang could tell—did not move from their spots. Jiang examined them closely; they bore their father's silver eyes, with hair of bright red. In their blue and green robes, they reminded him of the sky and the land amid pillows of clouds.

The sorcerer approached Jiang in a flurry, his silver cape rushing behind him. He held out his hand, just like Solana did earlier.

Jiang stared at it again. "What do you want me to do with that?"

"Ah! Yes! You are unfamiliar with this greeting, isn't that so? Here!" The sorcerer grabbed Jiang's hand and shook it. "Name's Othar. Odo Othar. But you can call me Odo if you wanna."

"Nice to meet you, Mr. Othar." Jiang pulled his hand back from the sorcerer.

The sorcerer, with a spin of his silver cloak, raced over to Solana's side. It was an odd sight; such a stark woman with an eccentric man. But Solana accepted Othar's kiss with a smirk.

Was that how people saw Jiang and Kikyo? An odd sight?

It doesn't matter. Jiang reminded himself as he placed the crate on the ground. He pried open the top to present the wine to Othar.

"Ah! Is that my juice!?" Othar rushed back to Jiang's side. "Ah, yes! I see! Delicious!"

"Yes, it is your wine. I have here—"

"I am sure they are delicious—oh yes!" Othar lifted a bottle. "We'll take your whole inventory—we want there to be enough for everyone!"

"I—I'm sorry? The whole inventory?"

"Yes! The entire city must celebrate. But not just them—we're inviting my late wife's family as well. After all, Solana will be Rosaura and Adaline's stepmother. Oh!" The sorcerer turned around again, his attention derailed at once. "Have you met my dear Rosaura," he pointed to the teenage girl in blue, "and Adaline?" He then pivoted to the girl in green. "They're smart as they are beautiful. If you are looking for a wife, they come of age in six months' time—"

"I am happily married," Jiang interjected.

"Oh! Congratulations, my friend! I didn't know! She is a lucky, lucky woman, I am sure!"

"I like to think I am the luckiest of men," Jiang said.

"Very good, very good—well, I shall have Solana send the exact number of units I'll so definitely need. I promise, I promise—it will make you quite a rich man."

Jiang bowed once to Othar. His head spun at the revelation—they wanted everything! He would need to place orders with his suppliers, conduct inventory, and restock the Kursaal.

Yet, that didn't matter. They would be rich—their children would grow up with a legacy.

And not a single drop of blood had to fall.

THIRTEEN

A week later, Jiang received a formal request from the sorcerer for over fifteen-hundred bottles of wine. He did not care about the type, the fruit, or the quality. The offer came with a single number that made Jiang's mouth grow dry. It was more than enough to purchase a sprawling ranch outside the city. There, they could raise a large family...and perhaps even dabble in making their own wine with a vinery all their own. Jiang had studied the science of winemaking and oenology in one of Master Botan's books. It intrigued him enough—perhaps he could create the best delicacy for all of Tencauri.

Othar paid half the cost at once, allowing Jiang and Kikyo to secure purchases of the wine for the ceremony, as well as to prepare for their child. Kikyo sent letters to all their vendors, as well as their father, asking for bulk discounts and deals. When the shipments arrived, Jiang bartered with his traders and delivered the crates to the palace. Part of him felt like he was betraying his family—but what did it matter? He had a new family now.

A new legacy.

And as the weeks turned to months, his life in Sīchóu Shíyóu was nothing but a distant memory.

Kikyo grew with their baby. While she glowed with pregnancy, it tormented her all the same. She no longer had the same pep in her step, and exhaustion marred her eyes. While Jiang prepared the new guest room as a nursery, Kikyo sat in a chair, providing direction and vision for their child's future room.

"Be careful," she said one day, "I think there's a dead rat over there. Thought I heard it rummaging about...it must have died a few days ago."

Jiang found the animal lying on its side beneath the dress, as Kikyo said. He reached for it. *Shame. The thing looks old. Too bad it had to die in here and not outside in peace.*

Just as he touched it, the animal gasped, and it hopped back onto its feet. With a vacant stare and a lop-sided walk, it meandered back into the wall. Behind it, just for a second, Jiang swore he saw a small pulse of smoke.

"Strange...guess it wasn't dead," Jiang muttered.

Kikyo shrugged.

They saw no more rats.

Instead, if they weren't conducting trades or working in the nursery, Jiang and Kikyo sat in the Kursaal in silence. Often, Kikyo spent time listening to the world outside their home. Jiang never interrupted, letting her listen to the world undisturbed.

Some days she told him what she heard, but others, she remained silence.

There she sat on the day the formal invitation for Odo Othar and Solana's wedding arrived.

The guard knocked on the door of the Kursaal, delivering it personally to Jiang. He took the invitation in both hands, bowed once to the guard, then shut the door behind him. He walked over to the table by the window. Kikyo's attention did not pivot as he sat down across from her.

"We received the invitation for the marriage ceremony. It will be in a week's time." Jiang read it over once more. "He has reserved special seats for us at the head of the table...he wants to honor us for all of our hard work!"

Kikyo glanced at him, then turned back to the window. Her eyes trembled.

"My love? What's wrong?"

She shook her head.

"Kikyo...what is it?"

With a gulp, she spoke, "Have I ever told you why we left Koai?"

"It was because of war, wasn't it?"

"In a sense," she sighed. "It was because of my magic. My mother had a similar talent...and it got her in trouble with the authorities. She overheard the details of a coup...and the military found out. They...executed her." Kikyo wiped a tear from her eye. "My father didn't want the same to happen to me, so we traveled far away, so they would never find us."

"My love," Jiang dropped the invitation and embraced her, "do not fret. You are safe."

"I was—but...history repeats itself."

"It does..." Jiang recalled the stories that Master Botan had him read repeatedly. So many of them preached the same morals, preached the same values—and retold the same story.

Again...and again...

"Have you overheard something, my love? Do you fear they will come after you?" Jiang cradled her closer.

"I do not know. But...I do not believe we should go to the ceremony...for both our sakes and our unborn child," Kikyo said.

"And why is that?"

"I didn't hear everything...I can't ever hear what Solana and Othar say. But a guard was saying something about...about magic. They said at the wedding, they would make sure all magic knows its place..."

"What does that mean?"

"I don't know...but I'm scared, Mĭn."

He turned back to the invitation. The dual triangle seal stared at him. What could they be doing? Othar seemed like a decent fellow—a little odd but decent. Solana proved more difficult to read, but she couldn't be harboring any malicious intent—could she?

"It would be rude not to go..." Jiang said.

"Mĭn!"

"We have done so much—"

"I can't!"

"I know. That is why I shall go...but you will stay here. I will tell Othar that you are feeling ill. After all, you are with child."

"But what if something happens to you?"

"I do not have magic, Kikyo."

"What if you *do*?"

"I think I would know."

Kikyo turned her attention back to the window. She tilted her head to the side like a wolf as she listened. "Fine. Just don't drink the wine."

Fourteen

Kikyo never elaborated on the wine. Soon after eavesdropping on the palace, she fell ill with a series of migraines that left her in bed for the week leading up to the ceremony. Jiang stayed by her side, even closing the Kursaal so he could tend to her every wish. Their child still had over two months before arrival, and any illness or wrong move threatened their budding family.

On the day of the ceremony, Jiang watched from the open window as a parade of decorated citizens hurried to the palace. Music echoed behind them, with a gentle wind catching papers on the table on the far side of the room. He straightened out the edge of his robe, then glanced back at Kikyo, still lying on the bed.

"My love?" He approached her, taking her warm hand. "Kikyo?"

She opened her eyes. "Hi, Mǐn."

"Today is the wedding."

"Go then."

"You are ill. I cannot. Surely Othar will understand—"

"You should go."

"Are you sure?"

"You said it yourself. It would be rude not to..." she winced. "Go."

"My love."

"Go. Just promise you won't drink the wine."

"You've said that before. What do you mean?"

"The wine...Don't drink it. I overheard a guard say that they won't drink it. So I don't think you should drink it either."

Her voice echoed with sincerity. Jiang knew he should not argue. So he accepted the plea.

"Very well, I shall not drink the wine. I can wait until I come home." Jiang kissed Kikyo's forehead. "Be well, my love. I won't be long."

Jiang arrived at the ceremony late, standing towards the back of the audience so he could neither hear nor see what had occurred. Othar and Solana stood at the altar, where the same officiant who married Jiang and Kikyo performed the ceremony. He preached about the gods and the promise of forever. Jiang didn't recognize the gods they mentioned. He only knew of Xiao Gui, who he had last prayed to when he left home.

But what good was a god when fortune had blessed him with everything?

The ceremony dragged on, with the formalities echoing. A baby cried. A child ran down the aisle. Old men yawned.

All waited for the festivities to commence.

With the ceremonial kiss and a final bow, Othar and Solana entered their lifelong promise of matrimony. They walked down the aisle, arms laced together, leading the way to the plaza beneath the donjon of the palace. There, hundreds of tables waited, with neatly organized plates, with cups of wine positioned beside each serving.

Jiang waded through the crowd to his seat at the table of honorees. He didn't recognize anyone beside him except for the space meant for Kikyo. Once again, a stranger in his own city, he sat in silence as the thousands of civilians took their seats at the table.

On a platform above the plaza, Othar and Solana stood above the feast. The daughters, Rosaura and Adaline, watched from behind the newlyweds, still as statues, clad in their usual blue and green.

No one spoke as Othar waved to his patrons. A captured his face, lighting his silver eyes.

Beside him, Solana raised her glass of wine.

Everyone followed.

Then she took a sip.

And everyone did the same.

Except Jiang.

He waited. For what? He didn't know.

Don't drink the wine. Kikyo's voice echoed. He trusted her—more than anyone. Over the last couple of years, she was his everything. Without her, did he even have direction in life? Did he have anything at all?

Jiang held the glass over his lips, pretending to drink with the others. He watched as the individual across from him took a long sip, then closed their eyes as if analyzing each of the unique flavors. While Jiang sat there with the glass above his lips, he sniffed it once. While it was obviously chardonnay, an unidentifiable and pungent odor breathed from the cup. He wrinkled his nose, then dumped the wine on the floor.

As he lowered the glass, he glanced again at the individual sitting in front of him. Their eyes twitched, and cheeks paled. Their hands shook.

And the glass tumbled to the floor.

Followed by their body.

Jiang froze. Around him, bodies continued to drop like flies.

And as they fell, yellow smoke filled the air.

Jiang glanced toward Othar and Solana. The newly-weds remained standing while their daughters slumped in the chairs beside them. Yellow smoke mushroomed from the area around Othar's and Solana's feet.

Slowly, the sorcerer turned his attention in Jiang's direction.

His instincts jumped in, forcing Jiang to fall to the floor, feigning his equal demise. The others on the ground still breathed while a single child cried in the distance. No one moved.

Silence hailed.

With his elbows, he moved along the floor. Each breath echoed, his heartbeat ringing in his ears. The fog grew thicker with every passing moment. What did this all mean? What was happening?

He couldn't figure it out. It had all happened at once. Did they do something to his wine? Was it a bad batch? Or was some evil magic afoot?

Every gasp of breath, every piece of fallen silverware, it all might have been thunder. A storm brewed around him, and he didn't dare look to see when it might clear.

Keep going. No one knows you're here.

He crawled past a woman lying on the ground. As the yellow smoke passed over her, she convulsed and choked. Her eyes flew open as she gasped out. A scream ripped open her mouth as her body paled and her eyes bugged.

The scream raced through the air, sending the birds flying and Jiang's heartbeat silent.

After what felt like forever, it stopped.

Her body fell with a final breath.

Jiang crawled towards her to search for a pulse.

As he touched her lifeless skin, another scream ripped from a nearby civilian.

Then another.

And another.

"What's happening?" Jiang whispered. Had his wine done this to them? Or the yellow smoke? Why was this happening? When would it end?

It didn't matter.

Nothing mattered.

Except for one thing.

"Oh, no..." Jiang climbed to his feet and raced through the falling bodies. If anyone saw him, he didn't care.

He had one thing and one thing only on his mind.

He had to get home.

For his everything.

His Kikyo.

FIFTEEN

Jiang had never run so fast in his life. The yellow smoke followed behind him, whipping through the air. It choked him on every breath, causing his hair to unravel as he sped through the vacant streets. No one loitered; he only passed a few unconscious bodies of vagrants lying on the street and rats scurrying between them.

Jiang hopped over each one. In the yellow smoke, the Kursaal's windows glowed like the eyes of a beast watching him. More shrieks howled down the street. *This has to be a nightmare. It's unreal.*

Magic cannot do this.

Nothing can do this.

The wine had to be poisoned, but the smoke and the death belonged to the imagination When he turned a corner, for a moment, he thought a monster waited for him, only for it to disappear in one blink. His ability to discern fact from fiction had been compromised.

Now the Kursaal might have been a monster itself.

He braced himself as he pushed the door open. Would he dare exit once he entered? Would the monster gobble him whole?

He shook his head. Wasn't he more rational than that?

The Kursaal greeted him, as empty as he had left it. He hopped over a table and raced up the stairs to the small apartment above the gambling house. The door didn't budge as he turned the knob.

"Kikyo! Open up! It's me! We have to leave!"

No response.

"Kikyo!"

Jiang cursed under his breath and backed away from the door. He clenched his hands, then rammed his whole body into the door.

The fixture fell forward, broke off its hinges, and slammed into the floor. Jiang took no time to collect himself, stumbling forward and racing into his little home.

"Kikyo!" he shouted as he checked each room. No response echoed back, causing his throat to tighten.

Where was she? Usually, she greeted him at the door. But not now.

He checked each of the empty bedrooms before ducking into the kitchen.

There, his heart fell to his stomach...

His knees fell to the floor...

And his voice rose to the ceiling.

The room spun around him, and his eyes fixated on the open window on the far wall. Yellow smoke dripped onto the floor.

There, it wrapped around Kikyo's body.

Nothing more than a corpse.

SIXTEEN

Jiang did not leave his spot by the wall as the undertaker took Kikyo's body away from him.

With her life stolen, his unborn child never breathed.

And with her life gone, Jiang alone wrote a letter to her father.

He stared at the paper for hours, debating how to formulate what had happened. She was fine before he left for the wedding ceremony.

But now...she was gone.

Just a numerical figure on the tally for all the deaths that happened that day.

Jiang heard whispers in his Kursaal. People called it the Yellow Hibernation. With most of the city put to sleep beneath the power of some poignant wine, yellow smoke plagued the citizens and eliminated the weakest.

Or, as others believed, it destroyed those with magic.

Jiang didn't care. It didn't matter.

Kikyo was gone.

And all he could write was "I am sorry" to Master Botan.

A week after the events, the undertaker laid Kikyo's embalmed body to rest in a stone grave alongside the other victims of the Yellow Hibernation. Jiang watched from afar, holding a flask filled with cheap wine close to his chest. He scowled with every taste. Its bitterness and foul odor did enough to quell his emotions.

His tears had dried up with Kikyo's heart.

"Please, Xiao Gui, take care of her and my child. Let them be free," he mumbled before taking another swig.

"I'm sure they will," a voice responded.

He turned in a flurry. A woman with blonde hair and a paint-stained smock stood beside him. He hadn't noticed her approach but could only assume that she was there to say goodbye to a loved one.

Jiang huffed and turned away from the woman, taking no regard when she left her spot beside him.

With Kikyo gone, Jiang moved in a haze. The Kursaal became his new home; with release in a chalice of wine, and a hit of adrenaline with each misplaced bet, he became nothing more than a drunkard in his musty gambling house. The Kursaal changed with him. With each passing day, the once pristine tables took a bath in dust, and the bottles on the walls glistened with emptiness. Jiang had no desire to meet with traders. His home and life became tables, the wines, and the cards and dice.

He slept behind the bar, too afraid to return to his home above the Kursaal.

He had nothing.

At least the wine and liquor provided a temporary reprieve.

But even that did not stop the pain in his heart.

The Kursaal brought conversation. People whispered about the deaths, speculating about what might be the next plague to destroy the city. What caused it? Who was responsible?

The sorcerer? His wife? An unknown power? Was it someone from Sīchóu Shíyóu? Or another opposition?

And what about the wine? Who procured it? Where did it come from?

The questions ripped through the Kursaal each night. Jiang humored none of them, drifting in his own puddle of liquid lamentation.

Of course, they would search for a scapegoat, though. That much Jiang was certain.

So it didn't come as a surprise when the sorcerer's guard knocked on the door to the Kursaal one night. He answered without flinching, staring down at the cohort gathered before him. With over fifteen guards armed with ropes and swords, they had prepared themselves to fight an evil giant.

"Jiang Mǐn?" the guard at the front asked.

"Yes," Jiang replied.

"You are under arrest for supplying poisoned wine to the sorcerer. Please come with us." The guard gripped his sword as if ready for a battle.

But Jiang did not argue, nor did he fight. He held his hands out for the restraints, his gaze falling far past the tops of the guards' heads. "Very well. Do as you must. I have nothing left here."

SEVENTEEN

The guard paraded Jiang through town before locking him in a dungeon deep beneath the palace. But for the irregular food delivery and the occasional rat, no one visited. Jiang was left to rot in his own filth. Light became a sparing blessing, peeking in from the door down the hall. No one told Jiang his sentence or his future.

Not that he cared.

The days turned to weeks.

Or was it months?

It all blended together, a constant fog of uncertainty.

In that time, he rarely touched his food, dreaming instead of being alongside Kikyo again. Perhaps in death, he would feel her touch, taste her lips, and inhale her flowery perfume. So he lay there, on the ground, without touching his food, and barely drinking his water. Sobriety came with hunger pangs. Any of the liquid happiness that had kept him afloat outside of the prison vanished, replaced with his sinking pain.

And he reveled in it.

Accepted it.

Perhaps this was all his fault. What if he didn't deliver the wine? What if he had never met Kikyo? Would she still be alive?

Or would that horrible sorcerer still have found a way with his magic?

Whatever the sorcerer's reasons, it didn't matter.

Now, under his power, Tencauri collapsed. People died.

Kikyo died.

And that truth, Jiang held in his heart.

Kikyo was gone.

And he would join her soon enough.

He stopped eating, pushing the food to the far corner of the room, letting rats take it away in excited hops. Rats at least forgot; they ate, they bred, they died. What made him better than a rat? Was it that he stood on two legs? That he could drink wine or think rational thoughts? Perhaps being a rat would be better. They did not bear the weight of truth on their shoulders.

Eat. Breed. Sleep.

Die.

Die...

Die...

Often he woke to the bodies of rats sleeping beside him. He poked them. Some woke with a startle, while others lay as if dead. After he stared at them for a moment and poked their heads, they would wake, though, gasping before scurrying off in a lopsided run.

At least they could die in peace.

All the while, Jiang prayed to Xiao Gui for death. Why wouldn't Othar just execute him, make an example of him, and carry on his way?

Instead, he forced Jiang to stay.

Rot.

Pray.

Can't you at least give me wine? Jiang thought as he leaned against the wall, unsure how long time had passed. The food rotted in the corner, and flies hovered around the stench. A delicate yellow smoke drifted through the cells, staining the air with rotting eggs. The rats viscerally reacted, stealing food and cheering with each revolting stench. Were they growing plumper? Hadn't the rats been scrawny the last time Jiang checked?

It didn't matter.

Nothing mattered.

Not his fellow prisoners.

Not the guards.

Everything blended into the stone.

Except twice, when a woman with blonde hair and a purple dress waltzed past his cell. She said nothing, humming an incomprehensible tune under her breath before vanishing like a ghost down the aisle. Something seemed familiar about her. But where had she come from? And why here?

It must have been a dream.

Nothing more.

Nothing less.

A dream...

A vision...

Or perhaps...a nightmare.

Eighteen

The story repeated.
On and on...
She was there.
Then not.
And Jiang watched.
Her last breath.
Her last blink.
Her last smile.
On and on...
Nothing else.
Nothing more.
Just him.
Watching.
Again...
And again...

She died.
She breathed.
She smiled.
She cried.
She died.
It never stopped.
No peace.
No rest.
Nothing.
A heartbeat.
A buzzing ear.
A single gasp.
Then nothing...
Nothing...
Nothing...
Until she died again.
And everything repeated once more.

NINETEEN

Jiang woke with a jolt. His heart climbed into his throat, and with the final strands of that nightmare, he rolled over to gag. His head spun as if he were locked in a permanent state of inebriation. When he closed his eyes, he saw Kikyo...dead.

Dead. Always dead.

Her soul, gone, nothing but dead.

He pressed his head against the wall. A rat ran past his knees, squeaking. Its ears perked up at the sound of Jiang's breathing, then turned its head to the cell door. Voices echoed down the hallway outside the cell, but Jiang didn't bother to look. Another prisoner? Another guard? What did it matter?

Let me be dead.

Yet his heart kept beating. His ears kept throbbing. And the rat scurried back into its hiding place.

His memories remained, a stain on his consciousness, beating down any sense of reason or logic.

Kikyo...

Her name cursed him.

Her memory left him broken.

Kikyo...

His mind screamed for her so loud that he did not even hear footsteps approaching until voices rumbled right outside of his door.

"Looks like there is someone in here," one voice said in Sīchóu Shíyóu rather than Yilkan.

Jiang picked at the wall. It had to be in his mind. Why bother humoring delusions?

Yet, could a delusion open the cell?

The lock clattered behind him. Footsteps rattled the floor, stampeding and shaking.

Finally, Jiang glanced over his shoulder.

But the newcomers, towering to the ceiling as giants clad in the uniforms of the Sīchóu Shíyóu army, did not approach him. Instead, they wandered to the opposite end of the cell, where a body lay on the floor.

Jiang froze. "Who is that?"

The newcomers didn't reply.

"Answer me! He wasn't here yesterday--"

"Dead," one newcomer said. "Must've been dead for a week now. Shame. If he waited a bit longer, he'd be a free man."

"Is he one of ours? He's got the build of a giant." The second newcomer asked.

A third individual, seeming to be the leader of the group, wearing a general's insignia, approached the body. He scanned it once, then turned away. "He was one of ours. Deserter, though."

"You know him?"

"Yes. He's my brother."

Jiang rose at the statement. The voice sounded familiar; the accent, the mannerisms. It was like listening to an echo. He pushed between the soldiers. No one noticed his presence.

Instead, they all stood fixated on a corpse. Maggots already nested beneath the eye socket, where bone and rot had made its home. Long black hair fell to the body's side. In some light, it almost seemed as though the body had turned to smoke and mist.

Jiang stared. *It can't be... I'm right here.*

One soldier poked the body with the tip of a sword. Nothing moved.

"It's an illusion!" Jiang shouted. "It's magic! I am right here!"

No one responded.

Except the general. His brother.

Jiang recognized Li Jie at once. Tall enough that he had to slouch to enter the room with long black hair and green eyes, it was like looking in a mirror. Li Jie was everything Jiang had wanted to be as a child, a fierce leader and a skilled warrior.

Yet, his brother hadn't crossed his mind in years now.

"Mǐn deserted my family," Li Jie said, unflinching at the corpse. "I said he would never join the army. But he didn't listen... and when he wasn't accepted... he fled our home. Guess he ended up here."

"I didn't flee! Father said not to come back!" Jiang shouted.

"At least my parents are dead. I won't need to break the news to them."

Jiang shook his head. Li Jie had to be lying. He had to know Jiang was right there.

"What should we do then?" the soldier asked.

"Nothing. Leave his body here. There may be others who survived Othar's plight."

"Yes, sir."

The soldiers left the cell, kicking the chains guarding the door on the way out. Jiang followed, mouth ajar. This had to be a joke. Why would they simply ignore him otherwise?

Or perhaps this was all part of his punishment.

The door of the cell remained open, and Jiang stepped, with wobbling legs, into the hallway. Already the Sīchóu Shíyóu soldiers had vanished into the next cell. Jiang followed at first, but they still didn't notice.

He was nothing but smoke to them.

Nothing but a forgotten memory.

TWENTY

Jiang stumbled out of the dungeon, squinting into the dim morning light. Whispers seemed to follow him as he exited, echoing louder as he reached the bright morning sky. Around him, rubble lay strewn around his feet, a broken collection of memories belonging to the palace. He had heard no commotion—but now, only a ghost of the palace remained.

No one lingered.

Even the streets stayed quiet.

The Sīchóu Shíyóu army established itself on every corner of the city, the giants brooding down over the citizens. Once again, Tencauri belonged to Sīchóu Shíyóu.

Whatever fight ensued, whatever battle took place, Jiang had missed it. The victors once again would re-write history—for better or worse.

Jiang traversed the city in a stumbling confusion. The city had changed since his incarceration. It was as if years had passed—it couldn't have been that long, though, right? The time in the dungeon had been a blur, but Kikyo's death felt so recent.

As if Kikyo had embedded herself into his soul, he eavesdropped as he walked, learning the truth of the situation to gossip and quiet remarks.

With no sense of time, he had lost over a year of his life. Weak, his bones cracked, and his skin flaked like paper. The sun burned as he walked, strength stolen and gone. In a year's time, Othar had both taken control of the city and lost it. The Sīchóu Shíyóu Army arrived after months, slaughtering the sorcerer in his tracks. His wife, Solana, disappeared, and his daughters, Rosaura and Adeline, fled the country without a trace. Where? No one cared.

War had a habit of marching into a city, staining the streets with blood, then disappearing in a gust of wind.

Jiang navigated through the empty streets, coming upon the familiar corner of his Kursaal. There, it waited for him with broken windows and an unhinged door.

Inside, debris lay strewn with broken bottles and tipped tables. A few cards and dice lay scattered amongst the glass. Jiang picked up a full bottle, still weighed by a murky red liquid, and broke its neck. Without even thinking, he poured the liquid down his throat. A cheap red from Sīchóu Shíyóu, but with enough alcohol to dampen his emotions.

He batted his lips twice, letting the alcohol seep into his core, and then threw the empty bottle against the wall.

Jiang maintained a life within his broken Kursaal. No one saw him. Not the appraisers that came to examine the building, nor the homeless that used its roof for cover. He enveloped himself within his bottles, drinking into an emptiness each night. During the day, he scavenged for food in the city, using his newfound invisibility to steal without consequence.

But in his loneliness, he could not escape whispers following his every movement. They came to him first when leaving the dungeon, but now they never stopped. Some days, they were quiet, but others shouted, begging to be rescued. From what? They never said. They just continued to poke at his thoughts and rip through his head.

Even when he visited the gravesite where Kikyo and his unborn child had been laid to rest, the voices continued their hissing.

With the voices following him, Jiang wandered the streets, breaking glass and emptying his anger by punching sacks of potatoes and rice. No one heard him scream. If he was dead, why did consciousness torture him? Why wasn't he reunited with Kikyo in some heavenly abyss?

"Where are you, Kikyo?" he asked at the grave where she'd been buried in stone. Time maintained its uneven dance. He didn't pay attention to the arrival of Sīchóu Shíyóu authorities or the reconstruction of the city. There were parades celebrating the success of General Jiang Li Jie and his army. Sīchóu Shíyóu citizens had returned to the city while those of Yilkan blood fled. Tencauri once again reclaimed the name of Tèrén Zhī, and the war continued without end.

Jiang knelt on the ground, placing his hand over Kikyo's grave. Bloody scabs covered his knuckles, and dirt calcified beneath his fingernails. Wine stained his palms. When had he last bathed? When did he last sleep?

He couldn't be sure.

From his belt, he removed a bottle of wine and brought it to his lips.

What would Kikyo think if she saw you like this? Jiang clenched his hands together. *She would probably call you some petty name and laugh. That beautiful... beautiful laugh.*

"Please...come back to me, my love," he pleaded to her grave. "I'll worship the ground you walk on. I'll give up my drinks, I'll—"

"Begging will not change a thing," a voice spoke beside him.

Jiang turned. To his astonishment, that same blonde woman he'd seen multiple times before, the same one with the stained dress, stood beside him. She stared across the crystalized gravesite. Her wide green eyes held an emptiness to them while her words skimmed the air like a cloud.

"You... Why do you keep following me?" Jiang snapped.

"Hm?"

"I saw you here after Kikyo died... and I swear I saw you in the dungeon. Why are you here?"

"Oh, I go where Death tells me. It is only in our nature."

"Our nature?"

"You're dead, Milo. Don't you know?"

"Milo?" Jiang spat as he said the name. "I think you have me confused with someone else."

"Oh no, Milo. I know... I know... I've been watching you, Milo. Good boy there...my Milo."

"I—"

"Come, Milo. We must report in at once so you can learn the truth."

"My name is not Milo!"

"You're silly, Milo. Come, come. At once." The woman beckoned Jiang to follow.

He stood there, gripping tight to the bottle. There was no reason to follow such a crazed woman—she might have been leading him to his final demise.

But what did that matter? He was already dead. What else could he lose?

Go. A voice that sounded like Kikyo echoed in his head.

So Jiang obliged after taking another long gulp of his drink.

Twenty-One

The mysterious woman moved through the city like a cloud. The streets contorted around her, and as she wandered, colors escaped her fingertips as if painting the air. Jiang followed in an unwilling state of inebriation. Something about the woman fascinated him. Her childlike demeanor reminded him of Kikyo, but the foolish sentiments reminded him of an overexcited pest scurrying about the decaying floors of the dungeon.

The city lost all sense as they traveled. Sometimes, the walls seemed to disappear, while other times, he swore they'd already passed the same storefront three other times. The woman giggled as they traveled, never truly acknowledging Jiang while never abandoning him.

Would she even notice if he stopped following her? Her attention darted about, humming disagreeable tunes.

But it wasn't like Jiang had anywhere else to go.

So he continued to follow the woman, who never gathered the attention of anyone passing them. Around them, the city had returned to its former self, with only the ruins of the palace as a permanent mark of disgrace.

Othar's name held no significance over the city.

History would remember him only as the mad sorcerer who drove the city into a curse of yellow smoke and death.

His name would be nothing more than an uttered curse.

The woman led Jiang to that history, though—straight back to the palace where he had spent his final days.

As they approached, Jiang took another long drink of his wine, then repositioned the bottle on his hip.

"Milo!" the woman called over her shoulder, "Quickly now—they are waiting."

"Who?" Jiang didn't bother correcting the woman again.

"Oh, do not be silly! You know!" she sang, hopping over a stone as they crossed beneath an archway. Around them, the remnants of the palace glowered at them. A gentle yellow smoke, wreaking of rotten eggs, drifted around the rubble.

Jiang gulped. Was Othar back? Was he waiting for Jiang to return?

He slowed his pace as they approached the stone stables, still standing at the back of the dilapidated structure. Straw lay scattered at the entrance. A bulky gray bolt guarded the mouth of the doorway.

The woman tapped on the door, "Oh Tom—open the door! I have found Milo!"

After a moment, the door opened. In the doorway stood a tanned-face man with a scar running down his face. His one good eye scanned the woman.

"Julietta, remember...Milo is staying in the north. He isn't here." The man said, his accent smooth like a cabernet from Gonvernnes.

"No, no, Tom—he's right here, see!" The woman motioned to Jiang. "It's Milo!"

"Milo?" the man recited, then glanced at Jiang.

"I am afraid your friend is mistaken," Jiang said. "I'm no one."

"Well, you must be someone if you are here..." The man approached Jiang, eyeing him closely. He then held out his hand.

Jiang stared at it.

"Oh, apologies. Wrong formality." The man clasped his own hands together, then took a bow. "I am Tomás."

Jiang still did not speak.

"Milo! Don't be rude!" the woman called Julietta nudged him.

He sighed, "Call me Jiang."

"Jiang. Very well. It is a pleasure to meet you." Tomás rose to his feet. "Julietta may have confused you for her first apprentice, Milo. Her memories can be jumbled at times. I apologize."

Jiang shrugged.

"But yes...you are here for a reason." The man leaned forward on his toes, glancing up at Jiang. "You escaped your nightmares on your own, didn't you?"

"What are you talking about?"

Tomás laughed, "I apologize. I may be overzealous, and you must be confused."

Or drunk.

"I do not think you are drunk enough to not know what is going on," Tomás seemed to respond to his thought.

"What?"

"Your thoughts. I heard them."

What kind of trick is this?

"I can assure you, it is not a trick. It is my...magic, for lack of a better word. It is all part of—"

"I don't care! Keep it away from me!" Jiang snapped.

"I promise, it is not—"

"I have no desire to get involved with anything magic." The mere word made his stomach crawl. Magic killed Kikyo. Yes, she had magic...but it was nothing compared to Othar's power.

Magic, uncontrolled, did nothing but destroy.

Tomás began, "Listen, I understand that you have gone through quite the ordeal—"

"I want nothing to do with this. Keep your blonde shrew and your hideous magic away from me." Jiang turned to leave.

The woman, Julietta, caught his arm. "Don't be silly, Milo! You followed me—of course you want to know the truth."

Jiang pulled his arm away from Julietta. "Don't touch me."

"Milo!"

"If I see either of you again, I will make you regret it. Go bother someone else."

Before either of the strangers could protest, Jiang stomped out of the rubble, disregarding the sulfuric smoke following in his wake.

TWENTY-TWO

As Jiang stormed away from the palace, the wind followed, blowing gusts of dusty yellow at his feet. He slammed his empty wine bottle against the wall as he wandered. He would have nothing to do with magic. If he was dead, if he was gone, shouldn't he know peace? Shouldn't he be free to live his existence without consequence?

He stumbled through the city. The retreat to his Kursaal took longer, with tiresome steps. He still hadn't reclaimed his strength, and after a few minutes, he slumped against a wall in defeat. What could he do? Where could he go?

Why didn't Xiao Gui take him away, as promised? What did he do to deserve this nightmare?

Did Xiao Gui hold him responsible for the poisoned wine?

"Don't you see I have suffered enough!?" he screamed down the road.

No one passing by replied.

He climbed to his feet and glanced down the path. Jiang had never been one for sociability, but he ached for at least someone to see him.

Did any of his old patrons wonder what became of him?

Did Master Botan?

The man never did reply to the letter about Kikyo's death. Jiang scoured the papers in the Kursaal for any sign of communication. Nothing.

Perhaps there was nothing to say.

Jiang huffed as he approached the Kursaal. A few appraisers circled the building. With no way to garner their attention, Jiang knew someone would soon steal the Kursaal from him. Even if he threw a bottle at them, they shrugged it off as some ridiculous ploy by the local vagrants.

With Sīchóu Shíyóu controlling Tencauri, gambling would be buried, and wine sanctioned through the wealthiest merchants.

Jiang kept walking past the Kursaal, strolling far into the far outskirts of the city. He could do nothing but wander, drink, and exist.

I want peace... The thought didn't belong to him.

He stopped. The whispers continued.

Take me.

This is not my home.

Help!

Someone, please.

"Who's there?" He shouted.

No response—not that he expected one.

The whispers continued their reveling.

Was this how Kikyo heard about the world? Or was he really just hearing the wind?

Jiang accelerated his pace. As he wandered, each voice continued its assault on his mind. He failed to shake it, no matter where he turned.

And they kept growing louder.

Louder...

Shouting for help.

He rounded the corner to the shanty town rotting against the wall of the city. People of all ages loitered, lighting fires for warmth and feasting on the scraps of food left out for the dogs. Jiang pushed past them. If he reached the wall, then he could leave the city. The voices had to stop once he was alone...right?

They had to...he would go mad otherwise.

As he ran, he tripped, stumbling forward and nearly hitting the ground. He cursed before loosening his foot from the culprit.

A gurgling noise ruptured behind him.

He turned.

There lay a body of a middle-aged woman, eyes vacant and mouth ajar.

As he stared at her, one voice screamed.

Please! No more!

"Leave me alone!" He pushed the body away from him.

Yet, when his fingers touched her rotting arm, everything stopped. The voice no longer screamed, and the spinning in Jiang's head ceased.

A gasp exited the woman's mouth.

For a moment, her eyes blinked.

Then they closed.

In that single breath, gray smoke exited her lips and congregated above her head. The smoke took the temporary form of a woman. Around its form, the yellow mist that had been following Jiang stroked her ankles and wrists.

Then she vanished, leaving behind an empty body without a trace of her soul.

TWENTY-THREE

Jiang stumbled, staring at the corpse on the ground. At once, his mind traveled to the stories of Xiao Gui. In those tales, Xiao Gui came to those long dead and let them breathe once more before their souls took a final bow. Wasn't that what just occurred?

But...why did it happen when Jiang touched the woman?

He laughed to himself. "I am losing my mind."

Stories existed in other cultures as well. He had studied them with Kikyo while learning about the wines. In the Leegan region, they had Kifo Kabaya, while in the Ainan region, they had Moltod. So many of these stories of death had been ingrained in their cultures.

And always, Death came with a calm, welcoming hand.

But they were only stories.

"This makes little sense," he muttered. It was a fluke. Perhaps Xiao Gui had come and gone at a moment's notice. But then...why did Xiao Gui forget all about him?

I must test this. He sorted through his memories; the voices started, beckoned for him, and stopped upon the soul's acceptance of death.

If he followed another voice, if a pattern continued, the same outcome would occur once more.

He tilted his head to the side, like a wolf listening to his surroundings.

Another whisper resonated in his mind.

I want out! Let me out! I said let me out!

Jiang headed towards the whisper, focusing on it with every step. He let it guide him to the other side of the shantytown, to another body, disfigured and covered with flies.

This time, Jiang took care as he touched the corpse's shoulder.

Once again, the body gasped.

Smoke gathered above its head in a humanoid shape.

The yellow smoke wrapped around its wrists and ankles, taking it to wherever peace loitered.

The pattern continued. Jiang tested it for weeks, wandering the city in a state of half-drunken interest.

Each day started the same. He downed a bottle, wearing away his sadness, then listened for the whispers. Countless souls entered their final resting place, leaving Jiang still standing alone.

Some days, he caught glimpses of that strange blonde woman, Julietta, watching him from the shadows. Whatever this magic was, Jiang was certain she had something to do with it. But he didn't dare confront her. Once he understood why he took Xiao Gui's place, he would face her.

At least, in some sense, the pattern gave him a new purpose.

It didn't matter that his Kursaal met its end. A merchant had acquired the facility and, within a week, turned it into a new tavern. The gambling disappeared, and only the cheapest wines from Sīchóu Shíyóu left the shelves. Jiang still visited daily to steal a bottle—but never left any form of payment.

The wine numbed the pain that came when he released souls. He could hear their fear and sense their distress, but within the friendly embrace of inebriation, it did not impact him.

Instead, he observed. Each time a soul emerged, they took a final breath and disappeared. The yellow smoke would wrap around them each time as if carrying them far away.

There was something strange about the yellow smoke. It lingered all the time through the city, a final remnant of Othar's plague. Yet with each day, it grew dimmer, its stench not so pungent, and the fear not so overwhelming. Its disappearance did not impact the souls.

Still, Jiang released them.

Still, they gasped.

And still, they disappeared.

Well, except for a few.

A handful of souls would remain, wandering past their dead bodies as if still alive.

Jiang first encountered a soul like this after about two weeks of testing his pattern. The soul, a young man with a flushed face, thanked Jiang with a grin, then wandered through the streets in a daze. Jiang raced after him, shouting that he couldn't stay.

But the man ignored him, leaving Jiang behind with the whispers.

In some ways, the dead man reminded Jiang of his arrival to his death. Was Jiang merely a ghost granted the abilities of Xiao Gui?

And if he was Xiao Gui, it meant he exhibited all types of death.

He learned soon that some souls vanished without a trace while others wandered with no shame. But some, a select few, never left their body, lost in a constant state of begging. Jiang would attempt to free them, but their bodies would never give him a gasp of life.

Trapped, forever.

After weeks of practicing, his confidence swelled. He could bring every soul to salvation if he tried. All of those hurt by his wine would finally know peace.

But now that he accepted the power bestowed upon him, he could finally save the one person who mattered.

Finally, he would see his beloved again.

TWENTY-FOUR

Nerves danced across Jiang's skin as he approached the burial site by the river. The crystalized sarcophaguses glimmered with incandescent light, holding each body in a permanent state of pristine death. A few whispered for Jiang as he walked past, and with a single touch of their tombs, they gasped one last time to meet their peace.

He took no time to watch these new souls, heading straight to the back of the burial site, to the tomb he memorized like the back of his hand. Unlike the tombs of the wealthiest, Kikyo's grave did not let her stare into the sun. She hid beneath its surface, surrounded by stone. He had longed for ages to just see her face...just one last time.

Jiang muttered a single prayer, then pressed his hand to the top of the tomb. Kikyo did not whisper to him. There were no voices, no calls. Had she been locked in her nightmares for so long that she forgot?

"I'm coming, my love. Please, call for me." He continued holding his hand over the tomb and listened for the gasp.

Waited for the gasp.

But none came.

"Kikyo…please!" He pressed his hand harder against the tomb. "Come now, my love. I am here."

Nothing.

Jiang stepped away from the tomb. Was this the wrong one? He had memorized this tomb—it had to be the correct one!

With sweat gathering on his fingers, Jiang reached for the lock on the side of the tomb. He fidgeted with it, listening for the snap.

He held his breath as he lifted the lid.

Threats of tears pricked at his eyes as the lid fell. Inside lay Kikyo, her hands laced over her permanently pregnant stomach, cradling their unborn child for eternity.

"My love, please, it is time for peace…" Jiang reached for her face. The stone tomb had prevented her from turning to bone, but her skin crinkled like old paper. Her eyes did not open.

"Kikyo, please...one last gasp for me, please." He lowered his lips to her forehead. *Please, my love.*

A moment passed.

Silence.

Jiang pulled away, tears threatening to overwhelm him. He swallowed again, reestablishing his callous demeanor.

Why won't she come to me? He gripped her hand one last time. Delicate, more skeletal than human, it snapped beneath his fingers.

And with that snap, Kikyo's body gasped.

"My love!" He released her, stepping backward, anticipating the mist to escape her parted lips.

But the mist did not exit her body. Rather, as she gasped, the mist gathered around her, entering every orifice on her body. It filled her, and her gasps continued, rising and falling in an uneven rhythm.

"Kikyo?" Jiang whispered.

Her eyelids fluttered open, revealing two gaping holes.

TWENTY-FIVE

"Kikyo?" Jiang neared the tomb once more. The body within it rose and turned its empty stare at Jiang. It did not speak.

But it still breathed.

"Kikyo? Is that you?" Jiang held out his hands to the body.

To his surprise, it accepted his hands.

"Oh, Kikyo...do you know who I am? It's me. It's Mĭn." Jiang helped her from the tomb. She stumbled as she rose, but once on her feet, she stood beside Jiang like a statue.

He brushed a string-like piece of hair from her face. She did not flinch.

Nor did she smile.

Around her body, a subtle mist pulsated.

"Kikyo, my love, do you remember anything?" He asked, taking her hands with care. It ached to look into her face with the empty eye sockets and dry, unsmiling lips. This was Kikyo in the physical sense, but something was missing.

Like her soul.

*I have awoken her body, but not her mind...*Jiang turned away from Kikyo's blank stare. It was like losing her all over again. She would never speak again, never smile at him, and never say his name. She would linger in this empty state, her body still holding onto a memory of an unborn child. Alone, she would fumble.

Jiang wouldn't leave her, though—there had to be a way to reunite her mind and body.

No, he wouldn't run from failure.

He would bring Kikyo home.

With night falling, Jiang led the corpse through the back alleys of Tencauri, back toward the Kursaal. The streets slept with disinterest, and despite the commotion of the Kursaal, Jiang sneaked Kikyo through the backdoor and into the upstairs unit. Transformed into nothing more than a storage space above the bar, Jiang had resided there undisturbed by the new owner. Each night, he listened to the gossip as he stole a bottle of wine. There, he learned his brother received a promotion to admiral and would soon herald the Sīchóu Shíyóu military in Tencauri. Jiang squirmed at the thought of seeing his brother, but that was the last thing he worried about now.

As he led Kikyo into what was once their bedroom, his thoughts only circled one thing: finding her soul. He couldn't care less about his brother or the affairs of some endless war.

"Look here, my love," Jiang led Kikyo to the dust-covered window. "We used to sit here, watching the city each morning. Do you remember? You would listen to so many conversations, then tell them to me while laughing. We could do that again if you remember."

The corpse stared empty at the window.

Jiang nervously laughed. "I apologize. You may not be able to see. But just listen...and here, touch the window-sill!" He guided her hand to the wood. Her hand flexed but showed no recollection otherwise.

"This was our home, Kikyo. Please...I know you are in there. Please show me that you remember."

Hope dwindled with each statement. The corpse showed no understanding of the surroundings.

Jiang slumped onto one of the wooden crates beside the window. Kikyo still stood there, reminiscent of how she spent her mornings. How many times had he woken, seeing her with an intent gaze, eyeing the city in awe? When Jiang woke in that groggy state, he loved just observing her, perfectly still, like a wolf hunting.

Only later would her spell break, turning her back into an excitable puppy.

And like on those days, the corpse slowly turned to Jiang.

He raised his eyes. "Kikyo?"

She held out her hand to him.

Jiang laughed, choking on silent tears.

Then he took her hand and brought it to his lips.

TWENTY-SIX

Jiang's routine continued. He kept Kikyo hidden in the Kursaal's attic, hoping that one of the old boxes might spawn a memory and bring her soul back to him. Yet, when he returned to the attic each day, he only found her sitting on the box where he had left her, having not moved a muscle.

He didn't fret over whether the owner of the Kursaal might discover her. Just like him, she was dead and part of this hidden world. Plus, there was no reason for the new owner to venture upstairs. The boxes contained remnants of Jiang's past, nothing of interest to some clueless merchant.

So he continued releasing souls from the dead bodies. Some days, the death toll overwhelmed him, leaving Jiang working deep into the evening. Other days, only a few souls whispered to him. Yet, no matter the number of passing days, he always asked for their help—could they search for Kikyo's soul and bring it back to him?

Even if they promised, no progress followed.

And Jiang returned to the Kursaal, stealing a bottle from the shelves to wallow in while piecing together his sorrows.

Kikyo did not comfort him, nor did she move. A shell of her former self, she lingered in their old bedroom.

And as the days turned to weeks, her body became less pristine. The skin pulled from her bones, while any memory of her pregnancy faded into loose skin around her belly. This was his Kikyo now, without her blue eyes and smooth skin. But he wouldn't leave her.

Not yet.

Jiang took little note of her rot until one day, upon leaving the Kursaal, his attention caught a conversation between the new owner and his apprentice.

"There's a foul stench coming from upstairs," the owner muttered.

"Must be a dead rat," the apprentice replied.

"That's what I'm thinking. I'll have to tear apart the entire place to find it."

"Others might eat it. We can wait."

"I'll give it another day. Otherwise, I'm going up there."

Stench? They can't mean Kikyo...can they? Jiang raced from the Kursaal and towards the marketplace. While he doubted they would find Kikyo up there, he didn't want to risk it.

There in the market, he wandered to an old table filled with potions, perfumes, and scents. Without catching the merchant's attention, he swiped a vial of peony perfume and placed it in his pocket. It was as easy as stealing the wine. No one noticed a missing vial.

Then he continued his mission in the name of Xiao Gui.

When he returned home that evening, he snagged a bottle from the bar, checking once that both the barkeep and his apprentice worked the tables. As usual, the apprentice flirted with a few of the young women while the barkeep rushed between tables, carrying bottles and glasses. Relief at his fingertips, Jiang then snuck back upstairs, where he sprayed the upstairs apartment with the floral perfume. A miasma of peony flowers encompassed the room, and for the next day, Jiang did not leave Kikyo's side, praying that the Kursaal's owner did not climb the stairs.

Once the day passed without intrusion, Jiang breathed in relief. For now, he and Kikyo were safe, and he could continue his plight to find her soul once again.

His quest resumed its wandering emptiness. No answers came to him. Even those strangers — Julietta and Tomás—never appeared again. Once or twice, while releasing souls for Xiao Gui, he swore he saw a blink of blonde hair and a stained dress. Yet when he glanced again, no one followed.

Instead, Jiang pleaded with each soul he released for help. "Please, return—" he said to them, "do not go forever. Find my Kikyo and tell her to come back to me."

The souls promised their help, but paradise broke every promise. There, they must have found peace—why return to the hideous world where people rotted in the streets?

Why help the man who released their souls?

*Ungrateful...*Jiang grunted after the souls vanished. How could they not help him? He could have left them to rot.

He asked for only one thing—but no one ever returned.

So he was left alone, returning to the Kursaal each day to sit beside his wife's rotting corpse and to spray the room with the floral odor of peonies.

The days blended. It all became repetitive. Even the taste of wine no longer excited him. His ability to differentiate the flavors had vanished, and he relied solely on the alcohol to numb his exhaustion. How long could he go on like this? When would he finally be able to sleep?

Like every day, after releasing souls, he climbed behind the bar to grab a bottle of wine. Yet, on that day, as he popped off the cork, he froze at the sound of footsteps above his head. He glanced around the Kursaal.

The owner spoke with a couple of patrons in the corner, but his young apprentice was not in his usual spot flirting with young women.

No...

Jiang corked the bottle and latched it to his belt. Heart pounding and head spinning, he raced back upstairs.

"Kikyo!" He shouted into the apartment. They didn't see her, right? She was part of this dead world.

But they smelled her.

Did that mean—

A scream nearly knocked him off his feet.

Downstairs, patrons began to bustle.

Stumbling, and with no time to spare, Jiang pushed open the door and raced towards his old bedroom. The apprentice stood there with a young woman gripping his arm.

The woman shrieked again.

"What is that thing!?" she cried.

"I—I don't know. I've never seen it, I promise!" the apprentice replied.

Jiang pushed past them. They flinched as if the wind blew between them.

Kikyo sat on her usual box, staring out the window. The apprentice and his girl remained frozen in place.

"Kikyo! We must go!" Jiang tugged on her hand.

Without prompting, she rose to her feet.

The young woman screamed again.

"C'mon! Now! We cannot stay here!" Jiang tugged Kikyo's arm, pushing once again through the young couple.

As Kikyo's arm brushed past the apprentice, he turned away, vomiting into the corner. Jiang did not delay, though, hurrying to the stairwell.

More patrons, and the owner of the Kursaal, had already entered the stairs in response to the screams. With Kikyo visible to them all, they froze.

Screams.

Gags.

Profanities.

They echoed through the stairwell.

Jiang saw no other option. He lifted Kikyo over his shoulder.

Then, despite the continuing disgust, he pushed past the gathering crowd, out of the Kursaal, and into a storm of terror.

TWENTY-SEVEN

onster!"

The word stampeded through the streets with cyclones of terror. Everywhere Jiang turned, people screamed. They did not see him, only Kikyo.

Couldn't they understand that she was lost? Sure, she was a rotting corpse, but she was still a human, searching for herself in an empty void. If only he could explain to them.

But no, he was not part of the living world.

He wasn't even part of the dead.

Once outside of the Kursaal, Jiang put Kikyo back on her feet and continued to lead her through the city. He took her through every empty alleyway he could find, begging that no one followed.

The shouts continued to echo. But with each step, their uniformity grew more erratic, more distant, and less organized.

Once again, the question returned: where could he go? Where would Kikyo be safe? Even the quietest corners and emptiest homes would not remain vacant for long.

Jiang hurried along without purpose. He didn't even pay attention to where he walked. What was he thinking, bringing a corpse like Kikyo into the Kursaal? It wasn't rational by any means.

Is this what love did to him? Did it squash his rationality, and now in his death, he was forced to accept the irrational. It wasn't like he had any repercussions. What would they do to him? He had already lost everything else.

He reached an empty alley and ducked behind a few barrels and tattered canvases. Kikyo did not make a noise as he sat her on the ground and covered her with one of the canvases. He then sank beside her, removing his flask from his hip and taking a long swig.

What am I going to do now? I can't put Kikyo back there. They'll find her...

Didn't any of them remember Botan Kikyo? She was the gem of the Kursaal. Even past her rotting skin and crooked smile, Kikyo remained.

"I'm sorry, my love. I've been searching for you everywhere...but your soul has escaped me." Jiang removed the canvas from Kikyo's face. He cupped her cheek. "I know you are there somewhere."

"Now, Milo, you should know corpses don't talk," a voice interrupted him.

He jumped to his feet. Smoke gathered at the front of the alley, and out of it emerged that blonde annoyance: Julietta.

"What are you doing here?"

"I heard a commotion," Julietta said as she approached him. "I did not expect you to be hauling a corpse around, Milo." As she eyed Kikyo, colorful trickles of smoke gathered around her fingertips. She raised her finger and gently pressed it to Kikyo's forehead. "Yes, that's right. I released this one years ago."

Jiang pushed Julietta away from Kikyo. "She was never yours to release."

"Oh, Milo, you're silly. Of course she was—I am the Mist Keeper, after all."

"The what?"

"You're one, too. Don't you remember? Certainly you do, with all the releases you've been conducting."

"You mean what I am doing for Xiao Gui?"

"Yes, a Mist Keeper," Julietta beamed.

"Then, if that's what you are...then you can give me her soul back!" Jiang bellowed, stumbling to his feet. "Let me see my Kikyo again!"

"She is already at peace, though."

"She is right here!"

"That is her corpse, Milo. Nothing more."

"She's still here!" Jiang shoved Julietta. She stumbled back from him, then vanished into a plume of mist.

He heaved, leaning back against the crates. Finally. Wherever she went, whatever happened, he didn't care. At least that pest would be long out of his hair.

He turned back to Kikyo. "My love, we must—oh, bull!"

Beside Kikyo sat Julietta. The woman poked at his love's cheek with her eyes narrowed. "Oh yes, this is nothing more than a reanimated corpse. How impressive! I didn't realize your magic gathered like this, Milo!"

"I told you before...my name is not Milo!"

"Oh, don't shout. It doesn't do well for you." Julietta remarked. "Besides, with that anger, you may reanimate the entire gravesite a few blocks from here."

Jiang paused before responding. "Reanimation? That is not what Xiao Gui does..."

"It is not the core function, no. But...if you had not run from us, you would know that Mist Keepers are more than just guides for the dead. We have talents and magic." Julietta raised her own hand. Around her fingertips, colorful spouts of mist painted the air, showing a distant recollection of Jiang standing amongst the rubble of the palace. Julietta continued, "See, I can paint memories out of the mist. If I have a canvas, they'll be permanent as well."

"Bull."

"How else do you explain your Kikyo's corpse, Milo? She moves, she walks, the living can see her...but she is not Kikyo. She is empty. Inside is but a blank void...with a body writhing in pain."

"No...she's in there. She must be in there. She held my hand!"

"Milo...look." Julietta touched Kikyo's cheek. As she touched Kikyo's cheek, the mist around her fingertips turned black like ink. "These are her memories, Milo. Black and empty. Nothing. Anything she has done is because you wanted it to be so. Nothing more. Nothing less."

"You're lying!"

"I won't lie to you, Milo. You are like me...and we must trust each other."

"No! Leave! She is something—she has to be something!"

Julietta removed her hand, then rose from the ground. She approached Jiang, cocking her head to one side. "I'll let you process what you have learned today. But once you understand, you know where to find us. We can help you put her to rest."

Before Jiang could respond, Julietta vanished into smoke, leaving the alley dark and empty.

Twenty-Eight

As the night darkened, Jiang remained beside Kikyo. He took her hands close, holding them, begging for a response. But she sat there with the blank expression of a statue.

How dare Julietta say that Kikyo was nothing? She was everything; she was light; she was laughter, and she was success. What was Jiang without her?

He lost her once. Bringing her back gave him hope.

There had to be *something*.

But in all rationality, holding her close, staring into her empty eyes, he understood the truth.

There was nothing...

Absolutely nothing.

Old me would have known at once... I never would have pursued this fruitless quest. He inhaled. What happened to the one who thought with logic? What sort of magic had befallen him?

Love...that's what has destroyed me.

He shook his head. No. It wasn't love. It was the act of having love and then having it ripped from him. He could never love again. Not like he loved Kikyo.

And not knowing the damage magic caused.

Now, with his own magic, Kikyo sat there as empty as a starless night.

"Oh my love, I am sorry..." Jiang stroked back a string of hair from Kikyo's face. "I should have let you go...you need to sleep. I am sorry..."

She did not blink.

"Come, my love, we shall fix this. You will rest soon enough." He held out his hands. Kikyo took them and rose. At that moment, she almost seemed alive.

But her empty eyes never met Jiang. Her lips never curved into a smile.

And as she took her first step behind him, her foot snapped and fell off her body like any old corpse.

Jiang carried Kikyo towards the palace, keeping to the darkest alleys and corners. Her head lulled against his shoulder. He inhaled her scent, trying to imagine her sleeping against his chest in the Kursaal. But the scent did not belong to peonies. Rather, a sulfuric rot perforated the air, granting him the single reminder he did not want to accept: this was not Kikyo.

The palace remained locked in time. It had not changed since he last visited, a permanent mark of Othar's failure as the leader of Tencauri. The only change existed in the form of a statue honoring Jiang's brother for his success and leadership.

Jiang spat at it as he continued deeper into the rubble. His brother hadn't even collected his dead body. *He didn't hear what Father said to me. Family never mattered to him.* His brother still occupied the city, at least the last Jiang had heard. But as long as Li Jie was alive, he never crossed paths with Jiang. For all Jiang knew, his brother might have become the new king.

It did not impact his life in the slightest.

Yet he couldn't help but wonder if his brother had ever married and had children. Did he carry the Jiang legacy? Probably. Did he marry out of obligation? Most definitely. His brother probably never knew love. He probably never had a Kikyo.

But that was all for the better.

The idea of his brother, or anyone for that matter, finding happiness and love in another left him nauseous. He would never cherish a family. Magic had stolen not just Kikyo but his legacy.

He wanted nothing to do with it. His magic reanimated Kikyo…but was it any better than the deaths caused by Odo Othar?

I shall never use this magic again. Jiang promised himself as he approached the dilapidated stables.

No. He would happily continue these responsibilities as Xiao Gui, but reanimating any other corpses would do no good.

Magic produced no good.

Even Kikyo's intense hearing did no good.

Perhaps it would have been better if Jiang hadn't known about the poisoned wine. Then perhaps he would have died too at the same time.

He could have joined Kikyo in her peace.

Or released her before Julietta had a chance.

The thoughts roared through his mind as he repositioned Kikyo with one arm. Then, with his free hand, he knocked on the stable door.

As if she waited for him, Julietta yanked open the doors in haste.

"Ah! I knew you would come, Milo." She exclaimed.

"I am only here because I do not wish for her to suffer anymore," Jiang said. "Please…help me bring her back to peace."

TWENTY-NINE

Julietta led Jiang into the stables.

Well, of what should have been the stables.

Rather, a dark, murky tunnel greeted them, dancing with smoke and dripping with dew. Their steps echoed as they moved, heading deeper into the endless stone walkway.

"What is this?" Jiang hissed.

"Our hideaway," Julietta said without looking back at him.

"You live underground?"

"It is where we are now. You know this, Milo. We move every few decades. Last, we were in Berusia to the east, remember? We moved here when Odo got the assignment, and we wanted to be near and close."

"Odo..." Jiang recited the name. "You mean Othar?"

"Odo Othar, yes. That was his full name."

"Wait...wait!" Jiang stopped following Julietta, eyeing her carefully. "What do you mean...you wanted to be close to Odo?"

"He was you before you were you, don't you know?"

"What!?"

"He was the next Mist Keeper. Shame his magic was not right..." Julietta sighed, brushing her finger along the wall. "But now we have you, Milo."

"WHAT!?"

Julietta didn't elaborate further, motioning Jiang to follow her. He huffed and obliged, despite his core instinct. The answer lay at the end of this path. Julietta would not be the one to acknowledge it, though.

Really, there was something missing in Julietta. She maintained a childlike innocence while speaking in tongues and riddles. At times, waves of rationality flew over her, and she spoke with unrelenting truth.

But there was still something missing.

A void, perhaps—an empty facet of her personality?

He shuddered and repositioned Kikyo in his arms. Her head lulled to the side, hanging off his body like a newborn who could not support their head's weight.

"Soon, my love. You will rest soon," he whispered as they climbed deeper into the tunnel.

At the bottom of the tunnel, dim candlelight flickered. Jiang froze as they entered.

Wreaking of rotting eggs and corpses, with the stone walls and haunting whispers, the memory of the dungeon fled back to him like an unwelcome storm. There he stood again, suffocated by his own nightmares. Julietta did not acknowledge the bars of the cage or the empty cells. She merely walked past in her usual daze.

But Jiang could hardly lift his feet.

"Why would you bring me here?" he asked.

"This is our home," Julietta said.

"It's a dungeon!"

"Oh..." she glanced around the room, "yes, it was."

"I died here!"

"No, Milo—you died at home, in bed. Such a sickly child."

"You're confusing me with someone else."

Julietta appeared to ponder, then shook her head. "No, I don't think so."

"Bull!"

Julietta laughed, then continued down the rows of cells, undisturbed.

Everything in Jiang's core told him to turn around, to leave.

But, if he left, what would become of Kikyo now? Would she continue rotting, suffering in his arms?

While he knew it wasn't Kikyo, just an empty vessel...he still couldn't let her suffer. Even without her soul, she was still Kikyo.

What sort of husband would let her rot like this? Especially after he was the one to blame.

He swallowed his fear and pushed back the memory of darkness. With each step, the screams of the dungeon came back to him, with the aching of hunger climbing through his body. With his free hand, he reached for the bottle on his hip and inhaled the drink, letting it wash over him for that moment. It brought him a sense of prosperity, one that let him become nothing more than smoke.

And there, nothing could touch him.

As they reached the deeper crevasses of the dungeon, the recollections only grew more powerful. A thick yellow miasma danced in the candlelight while the whispers echoed like migraines. Jiang's attention fell on a nearby cell.

His stomach contorted.

There, behind bars, yellow smoke loitered. But this smoke gathered in the shape of a humanoid creature. In some light, he swore he saw a face or a set of jaws. But, in others, it was nothing more than mist.

Staring at this strange smoke, Jiang's entire body froze. It transported him back into the Kursaal, where he discovered Kikyo's body, dead and unmoving.

Locked forever in a permanent nightmare.

"No..." he murmured.

"Milo!" Julietta's voice yanked him from the waking dream. "Come—Aelia is waiting!"

Jiang shook his head and glanced one last time into the cell. The creature had retreated, and once again, only yellow smoke remained.

It was nothing. Just a dream.

He pulled Kikyo closer, then hurried behind Julietta. She strode into an open cell, where the candlelight showed the brightest.

"Hello, Aelia!" Julietta said as she entered. "I have brought Milo!"

Jiang peaked into the cell behind Julietta...

Then he stepped backward from the scene.

There, sitting at a table covered in herbs and jars, sat none other than the sorcerer's wife, Solana.

Thirty

"You..." Jiang growled.

Solana rose from her spot. She still looked the same as years earlier, with perfectly kept hair, a skeletal body, and a stern face. A gathering of blue silk cloaked her, moving like the waves of the sea as she walked.

"Julietta," Solana said, "go wait for Tomás. He'll be back soon."

"Yes, Aelia!"

Jiang did not move as Julietta left, holding Kikyo tight. What was Solana doing here? Hadn't she disappeared after Othar's death?

How had no one found her yet?

"I suppose I have some explaining to do," Solana said.

"You suppose?" Jiang snapped.

The woman laughed, folding her hands together. "I never intended to harm you, Mǐn."

"Do not call me that."

"Oh, yes, formalities. I apologize, *Jiang*." Solana approached him, stride calm and even.

Jiang tensed.

"Please, allow me to explain myself," she continued.

"Why?"

"Because it will answer plenty for you, I promise." Solana continued her waltz around the room, hawkish eyes never leaving Jiang.

He glanced behind him again. The hallways had darkened with a chartreuse glow. Even if he did leave, would he even be able to navigate home?

"Please, sit—if you do not trust me after this, then you are welcome to leave. I will not stop you."

Jiang obliged, reluctant but unable to ignore the itching curiosity that pulled him toward the table. Perhaps this Solana would explain why fate had dealt him such pitiful cards.

He placed Kikyo in the seat beside him. She sat there, blank as always. Beneath the table, he squeezed her rotting hand.

Solana returned to her place by the bundles of herbs. She picked at a leaf, then met Jiang's gaze.

She spoke with poise and elegance. "My real name is Aelia Aseel. I am the second oldest Mist Keeper in our entourage here."

"If you're a Mist Keeper, then why could everyone see you?" Jiang interjected at once. No one had seen him, but Solana did not hide from anyone. Everyone had seen her face.

"You are quick to ask, and I shall answer." The woman placed the herbs in her stone bowl. "When you become more talented with the Mist and more ingrained with the dead, you can control it. I believe Julietta mentioned her ability to conjure memories, yes? And she also identified your ability to reanimate corpses? You must understand our abilities as Mist Keepers—or as Xiao Gui, as you call it—grant us a slew of magic beyond your wildest dreams."

Jiang grunted. *As if I shall ever use it.*

"Which brings me, quite nicely, to Odo Othar," Solana placed a hand on her heart. "I had faith in Odo...but for him, the Mist was far too much."

"Stop with the wandering thoughts and explain." Jiang hissed.

"Of course," Solana continued. "But I cannot explain without some background. If you permit?"

"Fine."

"Good. So, as you may understand now, there are multiple Mist Keepers. Four, to be exact. We have been given the charge of maintaining the balance between Life and Death. Julietta is the youngest. She trained beneath Tomás, who in turn trained beneath me, and I trained beneath Ningursu."

Solana paused, but Jiang asked nothing.

She continued, "As Julietta's time waned, we knew she would soon need to be replaced as the primary releaser of souls. The role of Mist Keeper can be draining, after all. So we helped her search for a new apprentice, but they kept failing. I believe she had at least eight or nine if my memory is correct. It may have been more, though."

Solana glanced at Jiang. When he said nothing, she continued her tale. "Her apprentices kept failing. They failed to complete their duties, and they succumbed to madness. We were forced to neutralize each one and imprison them in fortresses around the globe. We thought we might never find a replacement. Until Odo Othar.

"Odo had a deep inclination to the Mist. Since he was a little boy, he had controlled the Mist—in the shape of nightmares. By the time we discovered him, he was far into his adulthood. He had two daughters and a deceased wife, as well as a strong position in the Berusian and Yilkan governments. There was no way he could fail.

"So Julietta began to train him, but she was still stuck on the failure of her first apprentice—Milo."

"That is what she keeps calling me…" Jiang recalled.

"Yes, that one hurt her the most. Already Julietta has memory issues, but with Milo's failures, she fumbled further into her own confusion." Solana shook her head. "I stepped in, for I could not imagine Odo failing. Because of his knowledge, and his relationship with his daughters, we agreed it was best to teach him how to be a Mist Keeper during his lifetime. When he was ready, he would die and join us." Solana paused as if expecting a question. But Jiang had no inquiries, allowing the story to resume. "Julietta hadn't taught him much at that point. So I came to him as Solana—a mysterious woman that would guide him through his magic and teach him about the afterlife. He fell in love with me at once, and I played to his emotions…even accepting his hand in marriage and following him here to Tencauri.

"Each day, I helped him grow stronger. With my help, we decided he could use his ability with nightmares and control to hunt for magic that threatens the balance between Life and Death."

Jiang leapt forward, voice quivering. "Like what? How could Kikyo's hearing threaten the balance of Life and Death? Why would you harm her!?"

"The plan went wrong. We thought we had focused his magic—that we would find those who threatened our balance—"

"Oh, stop this lie! You used my wine—you poisoned everyone! And then there was no control." Jiang rose, gritting his teeth together as he bore down on Solana. "Tell the truth."

Solana blinked once, then sighed. "The plan, simply, was to stop magic. Not Odo's magic. Not magic from the Mist. But the unnatural magic—the type that has left the world tainted. Nothing good comes of magic. People die, the world suffers. Balance is unhinged. Your beloved Kikyo's hearing would do no good. Only harm."

"So you killed her!?"

"It is more than you can understand. I have been around for almost two-thousand years. You cannot imagine what I have witnessed—it must be stopped."

Jiang shook his head. He was never a fan of magic...but this? This was absurd!

"I have seen wars, I have witnessed deaths, and I have watched the world burn because of this magic. Odo was trying to stop it. That is why he called upon you—

because you could provide enough wine for the kingdom to sleep—”

“I wouldn’t have done it if I had known!”

“And I would have stopped him from asking if I knew you were to be a Mist Keeper too!” Solana rose to meet Jiang’s glare. “I realized it the day you came. I warned Odo that if he failed, you would be there to take his place. And he did fail—he died at the hands of the Sīchóu Shíyóu army and then succumbed to madness like all the others. So we were left with *you*.”

“You say that like it’s a bad thing.”

“You reanimated a corpse. That is not an accomplishment to celebrate.”

“Only because you killed her,” Jiang slammed his hands down on the table. Kikyo’s corpse flinched. After a quick apology, he resumed his shouting, “I became Xiao Gui, or a Mist Keeper, with none of your help at all! Alone, I was nothing, but it didn’t stop me. I am sorry that your Odo failed or that Julietta is a mindless buffoon who can’t train anyone. But I am here, I am doing my duty, and now...I shall leave!”

Jiang took Kikyo’s hand and helped her up from her seat. The corpse stumbled.

“We did not kill Botan Kikyo,” Solana recited. “Magic did. Magic cannot remain—not when we are the ones in power.”

Jiang clenched his fist. Why did she keep doubling down on this? He wanted nothing to do with her ridiculous stories. He would figure out how to help Kikyo...alone.

But Solana continued, "You're making her suffer. She will never rest—you harmed her more than we did."

"Be quiet!" Jiang dropped Kikyo's hand and spun to face Solana. Her dark eyes locked onto him, holding him in that pernicious glare.

"This is all on you now, Jiang Mǐn," she hissed.

"Enough!" He raced forward and slammed Solana into the wall. With all his weight, he held her there, fingers laced around her throat.

But before he could press down on her larynx, tendrils of black smoke crept up from behind him, wrapped around his ankles, and pulled him to the floor.

THIRTY-ONE

Jiang choked. The black smoke wrapped around him. It didn't feel like the yellow smoke in the cages but rather like a pair of hands pressing on his chest. He could not push it away, and as it clung to him, his thoughts grew murky and unclear. It was as if someone had pried their fingers into his brain, wrapped their grip around his desires, and then tugged.

His head seared.

And with a blinding white light, it ended.

Jiang lay on the floor, heaving, with Kikyo sitting beside him.

And above him stood that scarred-faced man, Tomás.

But it was not Tomás that caught his attention. Rather the head that sat in Tomás's hands. Half skeletal, half skinned, the head gazed at him with one blank white eye. The empty socket in the bone pulsed with black smoke while the jaw of the head opened and closed.

"So you are the one Julietta has been talking about?" the skull asked, its voice booming.

Jiang gawked. *This is ridiculous...a talking skull? I must be losing my mind!*

Tomás interjected. "You are not losing your mind. This is Ningursu, the oldest Mist Keeper...our God of Death."

Jiang half-laughed, "Xiao Gui is not some...*skull*."

"I was not born a skull. Events occurred, and I lost my body," the skull remarked. "But I am here now, just like you and your...lover's corpse." The skull's attention turned to Kikyo, sitting on the floor, unmoving. "I never did believe one of my Mist Keepers would master the art of necromancy...but it came to you so naturally. I am quite impressed, Mǐn."

"Don't call me *that*..." Jiang grunted as he rose from the ground. Solana stood, still as ever, against the wall.

"Very well," the skull—Ningursu—remarked. He followed Jiang's attention to Solana. "Ah, Aelia. You are dismissed. Tomás and I found Teodozia spending time near your hot springs."

"Where is she now?" Solana rose.

Tomás placed Ningursu's skull on the table and said, "Come. I'll show you."

Jiang did not move as Tomás led Solana from the room. They locked their eyes for a second. Jiang's body tightened as if being assaulted once more by the black smoke. But then Solana was gone, and he stood facing that strange skull with Kikyo still paralyzed on the floor.

Ningursu spoke once Solana and Tomás left. "I apologize for the difficulties you have faced, Jiang Mǐn. We did not intend for Odo to harm so many people...especially those who belong with us."

"Solan—Aelia has already done this song and dance. There is no excusing the behavior," Jiang hissed. "Odo killed countless people...and he deserved the death delivered to him."

"Yes, yes, he did."

Jiang raised his brow. *He agrees?*

Ningursu continued, "We had high hopes for Odo. We saw him as someone who could create balance for us and find the magic that threatened us. Unfortunately, he was overzealous. He enthralled himself with too much power. As much as Aelia, Julietta, and Tomás tried to help him, the power within the Mist overwhelmed him...and he used it for wrong. His demise was his own doing, and we were lucky enough to find you to take his place."

"You didn't find me. I made this role for myself," Jiang glanced at Kikyo. He became Xiao Gui on his own, trusted in the stories on his own, and brought Kikyo back on his own. No one trained him. No one created him.

No one.

"You are right," the skull said, "we did not find you. In fact, you slipped out from beneath us because we were too enthralled with Odo to care. If we had paid just a little more attention, we might have noticed the intelligent vintner delivering wine to our apprentice. We might have even noticed you in the dungeon when Odo had you arrested. But...we didn't. And for that, we lost the opportunity to use you for the greater good. And in that, you lost your chance to reunite with your Kikyo."

Jiang placed a hand on Kikyo's cold shoulder. She tilted her head to the side but did not acknowledge him. "You know of Kikyo?" he asked the skull.

"I know what you have done. Necromancy and reanimation—that is something even I failed to accomplish. But you have taken your will and your love and harnessed the Mist in a way to bring her body back. Perhaps if her soul still lingered inside, she would be back with you. But her soul is long gone, at peace with the Mist. That should make you quite pleased, Jiang Mǐn."

Jiang gripped Kikyo's shoulder tighter. It should have made him happy; that was true. But he wasn't happy. He was selfish and broken and just wanted his beloved back in his arms.

"She's suffering now, though...because I woke her," he murmured.

"Her body may be suffering, but her mind is blank. Take comfort in knowing she, at her core, is not suffering."

Jiang shook his head.

"You have done well for yourself," Ningursu continued, "but you have clearly come to us with reason. You need help, yes?"

Jiang closed his eyes and nodded. "Yes...I want her to sleep...but I don't know how."

"Then I can help. Please, place me in front of her...her suffering shall end in haste."

Jiang flexed his fingers and approached Ningursu. The skull weighed in his hand. If he tossed it into the wall, would it break? The question danced across his mind.

But instead, he placed the skull on the floor in front of Kikyo. Ningursu glanced her up and down, his single white eye piercing and wide.

Jiang returned to his place beside Kikyo. He took her hand, fighting the tightness in his throat.

"I know she is not here with me, but can I say good-bye?" He asked Ningursu.

"Yes, of course."

Jiang took Kikyo's delicate face in his hands. He pressed his nose against her forehead and closed his eyes. "Goodbye, my love…I shall see you again when I find my peace."

He kissed her forehead, then released her. A vacant stare remained in her eye sockets, locked in place.

Jiang nodded once, "Okay…"

"Very well," Ningursu unhooked his jaw and out poured that same black smoke as when he first arrived. It wrapped around Kikyo's face, traveling into her eyes, nose, and mouth. Her head snapped, neck falling like a rag doll, and her breathing grew labored.

Yet, just before it halted, she spoke, her voice like the wind, "Mĭn…"

Jiang's stomach fell. "Kikyo?"

But with those final words, her body slumped and hit the floor, a single carcass against the stone ground. One last gasp escaped her body.

Then no more.

She had returned to her peace.

"She said my name…" Jiang whispered.

The black smoke retreated, leaving him standing beside Ningursu.

Jiang met the skull's gaze and repeated, "She said my name."

Ningursu closed his eyes. "It was only a dream, Jiang. A residual of what you wanted."

"But—"

"She is at peace. Now you can find yours as well."

THIRTY-TWO

For over a fortnight, Jiang stayed in the dungeon with the Mist Keepers. He avoided Solana—or Aelia, as she called herself—but spent time learning from Julietta, Tomás, and Ningursu.

There was something comforting about Julietta's credulous behavior. She still called him Milo, but with her mind in spirals, Jiang held no malcontent. Some days she spoke with precision, while on others, she acted more like a child, laced with mystery and serenity.

Tomás would sit with Jiang, drinking wine and detailing the history of the Mist Keepers. In honesty, Jiang cared little about the wars and discontent caused by magic. All of that led to Odo, and whether it was with cause, it solidified a distrust in Jiang's soul. He didn't know what he distrusted: the Mist Keepers, magic, or something else entirely. But no explanation would garner his sympathy.

He did know one thing: he would never touch his ability to reanimate the dead again. The only thing that mattered was his duty; give souls peace, end their suffering, and continue.

Ningursu tried to get Jiang to use his magic, asking him to reanimate the corpses of dead rats in the dungeon. But Jiang refused. He would leave each session with a pounding headache that would send him back to the bottle and into a dreamless sleep. What good did reanimating the dead bring? Inside, they had nothing. Bringing them back would only satisfy some perverse desire.

Jiang spent most of his time sitting in the hallway, staring at the cells. He watched the strange yellow smoke batter the bars and listened to its howling calls. All the while, he nursed his wine, letting drunken memories of Kikyo haunt him.

Tomás joined him one day with a fresh bottle. He sat beside Jiang, crossed-legged, and poured a glass, allowing the giant to take the rest of the bottle for himself.

"No one has explained what lives in these cages..." Jiang said without looking at the Mist Keeper.

Tomás said nothing at first, following Jiang's gaze to the cell. He bit his lip, then whispered, "Personified nightmares."

Jiang furrowed his brow. "Personified nightmares?"

"They're what Odo used to destroy magic and harm your Kikyo." Tomás took a sip of his wine before continuing. "But they are more than that, though; they feast on the happiness of the living and dead. In some ways, they are the deadliest creatures in the world since most people cannot see them. It is just yellow smoke to most."

"Yellow smoke…" Jiang recited. He had seen the yellow smoke even after Odo Othar perished. It lingered around souls and followed his steps. But it had started with one person and one person only. "So Othar created all of these?"

"In a way," Tomás remarked.

"Seems like these cells don't really contain them. I've been seeing the yellow smoke around the city."

"It is the best we can do. Ningursu cannot destroy them."

"Why not lock them in a bottle or jar? That way, they're contained?"

"I would be tricky. It is not like bottling wine."

"No, I suppose not." Jiang took another long gulp of the bottle. As the last drop hit his tongue, he batted his lips together, then dropped the bottle. It rolled over to the cell in front of them. The yellow smoke waltzed into the opening and then strolled out.

Back and forth, like the waves of the river and the sea.

"It may be something to consider once we establish our next home..." Tomás continued.

"Next home?"

"We are nomadic. Often, we do not spend more than a year or so in one place."

"So...you're leaving Tencauri?"

"We have overstayed our welcome."

"But what about me? I thought you were here to help."

"We expect you will expand your duties beyond Tencauri. As you learn to traverse the Mist, you can release souls all around the world---"

"I am not doing any more magic!"

"It is part of your duty."

"My duty is to my...my..."

Tomás raised his glass of wine to the light. "Your what?"

Jiang looked away from him. "It doesn't matter. I am not leaving."

Tomás finished his glass and nodded. "Very well. We shall be here for another week if you change your mind."

"You're not going to stop me?"

"That is not my duty." Tomás placed the glass on the floor, then rose from his spot. "I shall inform Ningursu of your plans."

"As you wish."

Tomás bowed, then left without arguing further. Jiang sat in silence, running his finger along the top of the wine glass.

He couldn't leave yet; this was still his home. Even without Kikyo or the Kursaal, Tencauri had welcomed him after his family abandoned him.

While he may have been a Mist Keeper, he was an outcast among them as well.

He rose from the wall and approached the wine bottle on the floor. As he lifted it in the air, he noticed how the yellow smoke stained the glass. If only he could capture these nightmares in jars and let them collect dust on the shelves. But he did not know of their composition or nature.

It wasn't like wine. With wine, he could taste it, smell it, and identify its history.

But even if he bottled up the nightmares, they would all be the same: a constant reminder of his failures and lost success.

Thirty-Three

J iang left the dungeons three days later, despite Julietta's pleas for him to remain with them.

"Please, Milo, stay with us," she begged. "Your music is so beautiful; we cannot lose it again."

But Jiang brushed it off, leaving in the dead of night without saying goodbye.

The streets of Tencauri welcomed him back, the dead whispering to him so he may rescue their souls. As he searched the alleys and released their souls, he found himself lost in a dark haze of nonchalance. He didn't care who he released, how they gasped, or if they deserved paradise or darkness.

His attention only spiked as he came across graffiti along the wall of a walking corpse with a missing foot.

With long black hair and a blank gaze, he recognized the caricature at once.

"Kikyo..." he touched the image. Now everyone remembered her as a monster.

Would anyone even recall the happy daughter of the old vintner?

Jiang had wanted to leave behind a legacy.

Did he and Kikyo leave anything at all?

His wandering took him along the docks, where a curved ship with a wide sail bobbed on the surface. The different traders worked as always, counting their golden knots and securing their belongings. How many times had he wandered this path? When did he stop?

What would he be doing now if Kikyo was still alive? Would they have a cohort of children? Would they still walk along the water at night, recalling their wedding on this very dock?

He sighed and continued down the road to his Kursaal. Even though the streets had changed, the colorful exterior of the building continued its haunting memory. It disgusted him at first, but now...the Kursaal's beauty was only matched by a few.

He entered it without pausing, catching the deep aroma of the wine and smoke at the entrance. At the tables, different patrons gambled.

Did Sīchóu Shíyóu finally legalize gambling? It was nice to see the gambling back; without it, the Kursaal hadn't been the same.

As it bustled, Jiang moved to the back where the bar waited. An older barkeep sorted through the selection of wine with his back turned to the hustle. Jiang sat beside a drunkard, who rested his head on the counter, a tattered Sīchóu Shíyóu uniform cloaking his body.

"Here you go. Best one I got," the barkeep said as he turned.

Jiang nearly fell off his stool.

Old Master Botan stood there at the bar, holding a glass of wine. The old man looked almost the same. More gray in the face, but still Master Botan.

"What are you doing here?" Jiang asked.

Of course, the old man did not hear him.

"Go on. I promise it's the best I got. Those old owners, they didn't know good wine from bad. But now that I'm back, I promise it's a good one."

The man sitting at the bar raised his head.

This time, Jiang did fall off his stool.

His brother, Li Jie, sat beside him, dirt covering his face, his long graying dark hair unkempt and frizzing. He picked up the glass, just like their father used to do, and held it to the light. As he tasted the wine, he scowled. "Are you trying to pull the wool over my eyes? This is nothing more than a cheap Spinozan merlot."

Master Botan beamed, "Well there...you are only the second person to recognize that. Here, I'll give you a good glass...a true cabernet this time."

Li Jie huffed but said nothing.

"What is happening here?" Jiang asked again, still without a response.

The scene was like his own history playing out; Master Botan retrieved the good wine and placed a new glass before Li Jie with that usual grin.

"Only my late son-in-law ever knew the difference," Master Botan said.

"Hmph," Li Jie lifted the glass to his lips this time and smiled. "This is more like it."

"Good, good," Master Botan leaned against the counter. "Drink as much as you like. On the house. You look as though you have been through quite a bit."

"I suppose you do not recognize me?"

"I only returned here a week ago—received word that both my daughter and her husband succumbed to the sorcerer here. My Kursaal here belongs with someone I trust. So I came back from Koai for it."

"I see." Li Jie took another sip of wine.

"So tell me...what brought you to my bar here?"

"Let's just say…I took on more responsibility than I could bear…and when Lord la Halle returned with the Yilkan army, I could not protect my legacy. I lost my family. My post. Everything. I have nothing left." Li Jie grunted, then finished the glass.

"Well then, let me give you a place to stay for the night. Here we are all family," Master Botan removed the glass. "What is your name?"

"Call me Li Jie."

"Is that your family or given name?"

"Given. My family dynasty is nothing. I have no reason to carry it."

Jiang continued to stare as the conversation between Master Botan and Li Jie dallied. History dared to repeat itself; now, Master Botan could work with another member of the Jiang Dynasty.

Though his brother had abandoned the name.

In the two weeks Jiang spent with the Mist Keepers, Tencauri had returned to the Yilkan government. How? It didn't matter.

Wars repeated.

Histories repeated.

Death was inevitable.

Everything would return to the way it was as if Jiang had never been there. Kikyo was gone, but it didn't matter. The Kursaal returned to Master Botan. Li Jie had lost his legacy.

And Jiang stood, nothing but mist and shadows.

The Kursaal no longer belonged to him. He would be nothing more but a ghost, loitering and waiting, now more than ever.

Every time he looked at Master Botan, would he only see Kikyo? They had the same eyes, the same smile... How could he occupy this space now?

He clamored away from the bar. Every second hammered in the truth; he was nothing.

He may have served the role of Xiao Gui, but his legacy left no mark. No truth.

Nothing...

    Nothing...

        Nothing.

Jiang had nowhere to turn.

No home.

No friends.

No family.

He could only do one thing.

So he rose to his feet and left the Kursaal.

Thirty-Four

Jiang arrived back at the stables, his entire body shaking. He couldn't shake the image of Master Botan meeting with his brother. It was like looking into a mirror. If history dared to repeat, would there be another Odo? Would there be another Kikyo? He refused to witness it, not when the wounds were still raw.

The stable door opened as he arrived. There, Aelia stood, holding Ningursu's head. Behind her waited Tomás and Julietta.

"Ah, so you have returned," Ningursu remarked.

Jiang nodded.

"Oh, Milo! Are you joining us?" Julietta asked.

Another nod.

"I knew you, Mĭn," Ningursu added.

"Do not call me Mĭn. He is nothing," Jiang said, unflinching. Without Kikyo, who was Mĭn but a memory? "Just...call me Jiang. That is all."

"Very well." Ningursu grinned before he continued. "You have impeccable timing. We are leaving now for Leega—we identified a cavernous system in the mountains where we can live for a couple of years. One of my loyal ghosts is there preparing for us now." Ningursu motioned Aelia forward with his chin. "Come. We must move in haste."

Jiang stood frozen, watching as Aelia carried Ningursu down the path. On her hips, she wore a collection of yellow pulsing jars and bottles.

Tomás patted Jiang's shoulder as he walked past him. "You have some fantastic ideas, Jiang. We're glad you will travel with us."

Still, Jiang did not reply. His chest tightened while the weight of his decision crashed onto his shoulders. He was leaving with a group of strangers who claimed to be Xiao Gui. It didn't make any rational sense! Why did he act on this without cause or thought?

A hand rested on his arm. "Milo! Come! There is much to do."

He glanced down at Julietta. Her smile lit her face.

"Yes. I am coming," he replied.

She took his hand and led him forward, a skip in her step as they wandered through the rubble.

And Jiang let her lead him, wearing his emptiness like a badge. He would follow them—he had no choice. There were no others like him, and no one place where he belonged.

So he left Tencauri exactly the way he came: with nothing but his name.

Want to see if Jiang finds himself again?

You can find out in
The Life & Death Cycle

THE STORY COLLECTOR'S ALMANAC

Also by E.S. Barrison...

Tales from the Effluvium
Speak Easy
These Sanguine Tides

The Unsought Fairytale Collection

Heims Norte
Kainan
Rosada
Volfium
Heims Sur
Proveniro
Perennes
Janis
Frin Ayl
Sichóu Shiyóu

Map of the world at the start of *The Mist Keeper's Apprentice.*

AUTHOR'S NOTE

Thank you so much for taking the time to read *Nothing in the Mist*.

If you enjoyed this book, I would appreciate it if you could:

Review this book. Reviews are a great help to an author. If you enjoyed this book, please consider leaving a review online.

Tell Others. When you share this book with others on social media, you're allowing others to discover this story. Word-of-mouth is one of the best sources of marketing for an author.

Connect with me. If you want to find out about my upcoming releases, stop by my website at www.esbarrison-author.com or connect with me on social media.

Thank you!

E.S. Barrison

ACKNOWLEDGMENTS

To all the following, my thanks, for your support throughout this process:

First to Moira, my cover artist – this cover still leaves me gagged. It's gorgeous!

To Charlie, my editor, for your guidance and support. I couldn't do this without you.

To Matthew, since you're my husband I guess I should credit you in some way...and you do let me ramble, so I suppose that's good.

And finally, to my readers, I hope you now understand Jiang and his role in the *Life & Death Cycle*.

Without all your support, this story would not be a reality. So thank you.

ABOUT THE AUTHOR

E.S. Barrison has been writing and creating stories for as long as she can remember. After graduating from the University of Florida, she has spent the past few years wrangling her experiences to compose unique worlds with diverse characters. Currently, E.S. lives in Orlando, Florida with her family.

www.ingramcontent.com/pod-product-compliance
Lightning Source LLC
Chambersburg PA
CBHW060449300726